Lock Down Publications and Ca$h
Presents

I0658345

Bloodline of a
Savage III
WRATH

By Gritty and Raw Crime Novelist
Prince A. Tauhid

First Edition 2024

Printed in the United States of America

This is a work of fiction. Names, characters, places, and incidents either are products of the author's imagination or are used fictitiously. Any similarity to actual events or locales or persons, living or dead, is entirely coincidental.

Lock Down Publications
P.O. Box 944
Stockbridge, GA 30281
www.lockdownpublications.com

Like our page on Facebook: Lock Down Publications
www.facebook.com/lockdownpublications.ldp

Stay Connected with Us!

Text **LOCKDOWN** to 22828 to stay up-to-date with new releases, sneak peaks, contests and more…

Like our page on Facebook:
Lock Down Publications

Join Lock Down Publications/The New Era Reading Group

Visit our website:
www.lockdownpublications.com

Follow us on Instagram:
Lock Down Publications

Email Us: We want to hear from you!

PREFACE

Trevon Aaron Dietrich-Savage was someone who managed to make a grave transition from one direction to another—from high school student with good grades and a promising future upon graduation, to a drug dealer peddling light narcotics to harder products of high—then on to becoming a killer.

Von had a set goal established in his mind, and had long put aside (unintentionally) the specific promise and agenda he'd made to his grandparents (his grandfather Hound Savage in particular) and his mother, Lillian ("Lily") in the process.

A flame of greed and pursuit of power was ignited within Von, at the behest of the two cousins he'd aligned himself with in the dope game—the two brothers, Drip and Monk. The grandsons of Von's grandfather's first cousin (Methuselah "Mickey" Savage) were already thoroughly established in the heroin trade. Von needed the connections of Drip, and additionally, he desired to be one of the trustworthy figure heads of his, to operate as a distros of the highly addictive product Drip sold. The idea was to eventually carve out multiple territories to serve as distribution centers to get rid of the material. Von fitted the bill for what Drip was looking to do, not to mention the fact that Von's father, Cornelius Aaron Savage II ("Little Hound") was once close to Drip prior to his arrest and sentence of 360-month serve in federal prison. The two had made a lot of money together coming up in the game, and did conduct plenty of business. It was those same dealings that helped put Drip over the top financially, and afforded him the privilege to enter a different tax bracket. Von burned with desire to be like Drip, and took the long road to this destination without any regard for others who wasn't family or part of the crew he had command over. One murder moved on to another, and before Von Savage had turned eighteen years of age, he'd executed a few people—all head shots—and showed no signs of slowing down any time soon. He had first-hand observation of what true street power looked like and how it worked. And in his mind he had to have it for himself. And now that he'd tasted of that authority and rule, there was a want and need to gain more. But before he could reach the opposite end of the rainbow to gain a pot of gold, bodies had to drop, and many further mown down through the process.

When the going gets tough, the tough gets going. This became the mind-set and M.O. of Von, as he felt entitled and destined, to be the next street king of Philly—through blood and fear, as opposed to love and glory. The savage way for a *Savage* became the route he would take. He perceived himself unstoppable. Maybe he was.

Prologue

February 2009
Super Bowl Sunday . . .

The most epic day in all American history is Super Bowl Sunday of each year. Sports fans all over the country who love football, are accustomed to hosting parties to either celebrate the occasion, or to capitalize on it financially. Especially the gamblers.

The two teams who played that year were the Arizona Cardinals and the Pittsburgh Steelers. The Steelers were the pride and envy of professional NFL football in the Keystone State of Pennsylvania. They stood in contrast to the Philadelphia Eagles. The Eagles fans hated the Steelers and the Steelers fans hated the Eagles. In-state wars have been fought regarding the two. Death by killings have taken place behind them as well. It became an on-going rage and battle.

Several large-scale parties happened in Atlantic City New Jersey. AC essentially served as a neutral territory for Philly natives to place bets against Pittsburgh natives, when either city's professional teams were scheduled to play major games or each other. Philly folks dared not venture to Pittsburgh for obvious reasons, and Pittsburgh folks dared not travel to Philly for the same. The animosity between them was palpable.

Drip organized a trip to AC for he and crew to enjoy the game and other gambling events scheduled for the day. Alongside him were his brother Monk, his friends Body and

Animal, their cousin Kenneth "Kap" Savage, Body's brother Pervis, and another friend—Dreek—who was Monk's girlfriend's brother. Their first stop was to the Super Bowl party set to take place at the location. They'd arrived. Among the faces recognized by Drip and his crew was the host they knew from Philly. One figure stood out to Drip—a guy from the neighborhood, a friend and associate named Ahmad Saunders, known as "Rolla" on the streets. He was spotted conversing with a group of guys from Pittsburgh, all dressed in similar colors (mostly red and black), exchanging a secret handshake and communicating with a distinct style of street lingo and expression. They were members of the Bloods gang. Rolla was affiliated with the Bishops' Blood set, and the main dude from Pittsburgh he talked with, was a double O.G. from that set, known as "Brazy." Drip was acquainted with him as well. Rolla facilitated their introduction for a business deal before the day. Drip provided Brazy with four bricks of his heroin product. Another transaction was being arranged for after the game. They were to drive back to Philly to work this one. Brazy and his boys would swing through on the way back home.

Brazy was a die-hard Steelers fan. He was popping all types of big boy shit on what his team was going to do to the opponent. He loved to gamble as well. That was one of the main reasons he traveled to AC with $500K to play with. Despite having a substantial amount to wager, he couldn't match Drip's financial prowess. As for Drip, an avid Eagles supporter and gambler, he couldn't tolerate hearing a Steelers enthusiast talk big. Brazy was no exception.

"What's good, Rolla? How you be, my nigga?" Drip said as he dapped the guy up. This was his childhood friend.

"I'm good, Drip. You?" Rolla responded.

"You know me, my nigga. I'm up. And I'm always good. I'm really tryna see what's this Brazy popping over there about?" said Drip, now eyeing Brazy.

The two locked eyes. Brazy returned the same energy.

"Shit, my nigga, I'm poppin' 'bout what you poppin' 'bout. Me and my dawgs like the Steelers! We tryna put down some bread on a bet!" Brazy fired back.

"How much you talking, nigga?" asked Drip. "I'mma match everything you and your nut-ass dudes got to bet on them sorry ass Steelers, my nigga! Pick a number! You know me. My money long and Kingpin strong!" he spat.

"Shit, nigga! We got a hundred bands! What up?"

"Nigga . . . bet your re-up money you came to see me with! Make it two hunnid thousand! And when them no-good Steelers loose, you pay me that! Then, you come up with two hunnid more to buy your product with. How 'bout that!" Drip spat emphatically.

"Nigga, bet it! I ain't got no problem with that because, I'm confident my Steelers and Big Ben gonna demolish the Cardinals! I only wish it was them bitch-ass Eagles instead! I hate all Philly teams!"

"Say no more, nigga! Bet it up," Drip said, then put out his hand to shake Brazy's so to lock in the deal.

Brazy immediately grabbed his hand to secure the bet. They then got close to one of the many big screens that surround the bar to tune in.

****

Several Hours Later . . .

Brazy and all the Steelers fans talked big shit throughout the whole game, with him being the loudest among them. The excitement peeked when Steelers' defensive line-man, James Harrison, intercepted Cardinals' QB Kurt Warner, returning for a game-winning touchdown, securing victory for the Steelers. He was louder than everybody, even more so at that point. Now it was time for Brazy to collect his winnings. He and his boys began walking towards Drip and his boys. Brazy continued to pop shit, adding to the irritation.

Drip was now surrounded by his crew and many other Philly dudes who knew and respected his influence in the city. They far outnumbered Brazy and his Blood gang. Brazy's advance was halted by Body and Animal.

"Drip don't wanna see or talk to nobody," Body said.

"Yo, I don't give a fuck about none of that! Dude owe me money. He lost a bet," Brazy responded.

Drip then walked a little closer. "Nigga! I'll never pay a lame like you! On no account! I can lose a thousand bets but won't ever pay out to a nigga like you! So fall the fuck back! Sucks!" he capped.

"What! You gonna pay me mine, my nigga!"

"If you wasn't popping all that shit, you probably could've been paid a little something. But fuck that! You ain't getting shit now!" Drip lastly said, then he and his crew began walking towards the exit door.

"So it's like that, Drip?" Brazy yelled out over the loud music playing. "We gonna take it there about a bet?"

Drip stopped and turned to address those words.

"Take it how you wanna take it, nigga! Get it like the Red Cross! Or like the name of that wack-ass gang you part of... In Blood, fuck-boy!" he spat, then moved on.

Brazy took the insult hard.

"A'ight, nigga! That's how you want it. Have it your way. I'mma see you later though. On God, I am!"

Drip flipped the middle finger and shot Brazy a bird as he walked out.

From that point onward, animosity brewed between the two. Drip consistently belittled Brazy to his people, however he saw fit. He made him appear weak in the eyes of all witnesses to their heated verbal exchange. Brazy's pride was at stake. He couldn't let it slide, as no man would expect him to.

PART ONE

Chapter 1

Late February, 2009 . . .

The three-way relationship involving Von, Chloe, and Rosa, began to solidify at its core after the meeting with Tito. With that hurdle behind them, the girls felt confident that there would be no more family drama involving Von and their people.

While at work, Rosa often had lunch and conversed with her female co-worker and friend, Meadow Erickson. It was she, who so happened to be a white girl who looked and behaved like a female of color. Meadow and Rosa, being the same age, shared basically similar tastes and preferences in life and material things. They were two of a kind.

Meadow stood at five-six in height and weighed one hundred and thirty pounds. She maintained her hair in a loving style. Her brunette feature cascaded just past her shoulders. At times she dyed it a blondish-brown hue. There was a slightly wavy texture about it. Meadow boasted an exquisite tanned complexion, a fit body and a strikingly appealing way of dressing herself. She had a penchant for jeans, designer sneakers, and pop culture, embodying a mindset akin to *Chanel West Coast,* a female rapper who made an early rise. Meadow and Rosa often enjoyed shopping together on weekends when they were off. Such bonanza was on the horizon.

While working at the nursing home where they were employed, Rosa felt it was necessary to inform Meadow about the situation involving her, Chloe, and Von. Meadow had already observed the signs of pregnancy evident in Rosa's expanding butt and hips. Being a mother herself, she understood what Rosa was going through. However, she still felt compelled to ask for clarification.

"Rosa, you must be pregnant or something, girl? You've gotten thicker," she gloated.

Rosa produced a bright pleasant smile. "I am," she responded. "I was gonna tell you at some point. Was just busy tryna figure out how to relate it to you."

"Tryna figure out how to relate to me, *you're pregnant!*" Meadow retorted with a giggle.

"Mmm-hmm! Because it's so much to it I'm sure you're gonna be dying to know."

Meadow jarred her head and had a curious smirk about her face.

"Now, see . . . you got me dying to know now. We've got time. Our lunch break is not over for another forty-five minutes. So go ahead and get busy giving me all the juicy details. I wanna know how nice the dick was, the wife he cheated on, and what you love so much about his swag to let him release inside of you. Please talk to me, boo-boo. I'm listening," Meadow said with a wide smile.

The two girls were seated in the facility's cafeteria, enjoying wings and salad.

"You sure you ready for this?" Rosa mused with a charming smile.

"Rosa, you already know I am. Now stop holding back, please."

Rosa's smile persisted as she delved deep into the story.

"All right, so look. I have a cousin who is pregnant too. Chloe. You met her before."

"I have. But please keep going," Meadow urged.

"Me and Chloe got pregnant around the same time. But here is the most interesting part. We're both pregnant and in love with the same guy."

"Get the hell outta here! What you say!" Meadow exclaimed with excitement. "This dude must really got it going on, honey."

"He does. And in fact . . ."

Rosa proceeded to provide Meadow with a comprehensive view of their life and relationship. Meadow was captivated by the enchanting details of their affair, craving more revelations with every word.

****

Von's sister, Kidada, reached out to him. She was curious to know if or not he was in the city or up in Williamsport. She wanted to see him, mentioning that their grandfather, Big Hound, also wished to see them both, at the same time.

Meanwhile, Von found himself laid back chilling and enjoying the companionship of Monyetta at her place on a lazy Sunday afternoon, just past noon.

"What's good, sis? How you been?" Von answered upon noticing her number appear on the screen of his phone.

"What's popping, bro? I've been good on my end. You?"

"You know me. My mind on my money, and I'm being sure to take care of business the right way."

"I know that's right."

The night before, Von and Monyetta counted $200,000 of the cash he had from the work sold up in Williamsport. This was all his dough, as he'd paid Monk the money he owed Drip, and they were now ready to be supplied with more bricks of "Boy." The young nigga was definitely moving that dope with a purpose and a sense of urgency. He moved and operated as if his life depended upon the sell of it. All those goddamn babies dude had on the way really made him step his game up like he hadn't before. Although Von didn't yet disclose his reality to Monyetta, he planned to do so in due time.

Of the $200K, he gave Monyetta $20,000 of it, and was determined to provide Chloe, Rosa, and Cori, $25K each as well. As for the majority of the money to remain—$100K— Von intended to stash it at his grandmother's home, to be used when he needed it in the future.

The conversation continued between Von and his sister.

"Your mind on your money and you handle your business the right way. I know that's right," she reworded Von's phrase. But anyway, I was hoping you were here in Philly?" Kidada asked.

"I am. Actually, I'm at my sweetheart's crib. Her name, Monyetta."

Monyetta glanced over at him and smiled warmly as they sat together on the bed, engrossed in watching a movie.

"Oh, her!" Kidada said in a pleasant fashion. "She's the kind, dark-skinned cutie, right?"

"Ah . . . yeah. How you know that?" he let out with a laugh.

"Because . . . Pops speaks so highly about her. He said we sort of favor one another. She must really be nice, huh!"

"Yeah, y'all two do favor each other. Y'all have the same type of style and personality too," Von said.

"So when you plan to have us meet each other? I'm dying to see who this female be that got my brother's nose wide open," Kidada said.

"We can do that today, sis. Me and her gonna be relaxing right here all day."

"I'll definitely be on my way over soon. I've gotta get dressed first. And by the way, Grandpa wants to see the both of us, whenever we have a chance to go by. Today would be a good time to do so."

"Oh! He does?"

"Yep. He says we haven't been by in a while. Which is true. Plus, I wanna see them anyway. He and grandma, Henrietta."

"A'ight. Come on by. We can go visit them in your car. When we leave there, we can then go do some shopping or something. Or out to AC?"

"Cool. I'mma go ahead and get dressed and make my way towards you and this *Monyetta* piece I can't wait to meet. Text me the directions to the spot. And I'll see y'all soon, bro"

"That's a bet. Take care!" Von lastly said

"You too, bro."

The two siblings ended the call.

"Everything okay?" Moneytta asked.

"Oh yeah. Everything good, babe. That was my sister. Kidada's her name. She about to come over soon. We all gonna spend the day together. My grandparents wanna see us."

"This must be your dad's parents?"

"Yeah. The one you met before is my mom's mother."

"Understood. I can't wait to meet them. Let's go ahead and get up and get dressed. We need to get out and move around a little anyway."

"Let's do that. I've gotta drop off some money at my grandmom Enda's house too. So let's get going for the day," Von stated. He'd completely overlooked the fact that he was not only a wanted man for one homie. The cops were looking for him regarding two. He seemed to simply not give a damn.

The two then took a shower, ate a light meal, got dressed, and waited for Kidada to arrive.

Two hours later, Kidada was there. Upon her stepping into the apartment, Monyetta greeted her warmly. The two lovely young ladies exchanged pleasantries, shared hugs, and instantly connected with palpable chemistry and energy.

"You *are* amazing, aren't you? Nice piece of work here, Vonnie. I like her already." Kidada complimented with a smile.

"You're amazing as well, Kidada. I really like your style and the way you carry yourself," Monyetta responded, her face glowing with admiration. Kidada had an enchanting presence that mesmerized her. The feeling was mutual.

"What's that you rocking? I love those heels," Kidada asked.

"This is *Prada* here, boo. I'm a fiend for it. What about you? What's that you rocking?"

"All *Fendi,* everything. I can't live without it."

"Ooh! Classy."

"Kiki, won't you take a seat for a moment? I'll be ready in a minute," Von said.

The girls settled onto the love seat and delved into a deep conversation. Their tones were soft, fostering a sense of closeness and connection.

Damn! Them two are getting along like they been knowing each other for years, Von thought.

He took the $175,000 of the money and put it in the Gucci backpack he loved to tote around. Von was now ready to roll.

"Kidada, I'mma need you to make a stop by my granny Edna's house before we go see grandpa, Hound," Von said to his sister.

"For sho'."

"Y'all ready to ride?" Von asked.

"We are."

Kidada and Monyetta replied in sync.

They then exited the apartment and made their way to their destinations.

Chapter 2

One Hour Later . . .

The three arrived at the gated community where the legendary Hound Savage lived. The lawn of the home was well-manicured, and the hedges had a perfected architectural trim.

"This is a nice home, Vonnie," Monyetta said.

"Just wait until you meet the man who own the house. Grandpop that dude!" Von responded.

Kidada smiled at the reaction of Monyetta. She could tell that Monyetta adored the culture and mindset her family embodied.

Hound's wife let them inside.

"Hey, Nana." Kidada and Von seemingly greeted at the same time.

"Hey, babies! How y'all doing? I'm glad to see you two," Mrs. Henrietta said.

"We good, Nana," Von said. "This here my girlfriend. Her name is Monyetta."

"Hello, baby. Nice to meet you," Mrs. Henrietta greeted Moneyatta.

She hugged all three of them.

"Where grandpa?" asked Von.

"He in there watching the ball game. You know he loves baseball."

Von and Kidada both smiled at the fact of knowing how true that was.

With Kidada leading the way, they entered the den where their grandfather sat on the plush leather couch he favored. He was well-dressed and seemed like he was about to go somewhere important.

"Hey, grandpop! Me and Vonnie finally made it to see you like you wanted us to," Kidada spoke for them both. "And this is Vonnie's girlfriend here. He wanted her to meet you and Nana as well."

"Hello-hello-hello! Ain't I glad to see you two!" Hound responded with a pleasant smile, getting to his feet to hug his grandchildren and guest.

"And where you going? All dressed and clean like you got a business meeting to attend!" Kidada said.

"What's good, grandpop?" said Von. "How you been? Meet Monyetta. She's my future wife."

Hound's smile radiated a new-found warmth as he beheld the beauty and graceful femininity of the young bombshell.

"Boy! You got yourself something here, don't you?" Hound stated meaningfully.

"That's the same thing I said, grandpop," Kidada chimed in.

"She fit the bill of a keeper. He doing right by you, ain't he, baby?" the old gangster asked Monyetta.

"Yes, sir. He is. He takes care of me and treats me very well," Monyetta responded.

They all took a seat. Hound was sandwiched between his two grand kids. Monyetta sat in the seat across them.

"What you do for a living, baby?" Hound asked Monyetta.

"I'm in college, sir. For journalism. And I work part-time at two decent jobs. One at an upscale clothing store. And the other, at a coffee shop. Starbucks."

"You're so pretty. You got your head on straight. You headed in the right direction in life. And, you don't have any kids, I'm assuming?"

"No, sir. No kids."

Hound turned to look at Von like he was crazy. "Boy, what's wrong you! Why ain't you made this gal here your wife? She's the perfect one. If you know like I do, I would've married her. Because we need more marriages and babies in this Savage family of ours. If I have to, hell, I'll pay for everything. I just want you to make it happen!" Hound declared.

Von and Monyetta exchanged smiles. She looked on at him strongly while anticipating his response. Kidada, too, shared in the moment. Her gaze unwavering.

"We gonna get to that part soon, grandpop. Maybe next year," stated Von.

"Why not *this* year?" Hound asked.

Monyetta and Kidada exchanged glances again as they looked from Hound to Von.

"Because, grandpops . . . if and when I get married, I would want to do so in the summertime, while it's warm and vibrant."

"Y'all two can go down to Miami to make that happen. That's if you need a few more months to decide. But while it's cold here, if you make up your mind to do so in November or December, Miami will be perfect. Me and your grandmother in there, got married in January, down in the Cayman Islands, son. Just know your grandpa is rooting for you. You and this lovely girl here. Don't waste time, Vonnie, because you'll live with regret. And if you let this young lady here get away from you, that'll be a foolish mistake."

"I understand your point, grandpa. But you must have had a woman in your life at one point you regret not making your wife?" Von asked.

"I did. She was a very beautiful female too. A great singer. Her name was Sharon Tatum. She went by *Shugg Tatum.* That's two G's."

"You and her had something going on, grandpop?" Kidada asked in surprise. "I know that name. She's the singer lady who everybody compares to Betty Wright, Patti

LaBelle, and Gladys Knight. My mom's mother loves that woman's music. She's originally from Georgia, I wanna say," Kidada stated.

"That's her. You know I'm originally from Georgia too. But back in nineteen-fifty-eight, me and Shugg had a thing for one another. She was ready to settle down. I wasn't. The rest is history. But anyway, look . . ."

Hound continued his conversation with his grandchildren. His happiness evident as he cherished spending quality time with the youngsters. Big Hound had three sons and four grandkids. Three of whom were from Hound Jr.

The late seventies old world gangster absolutely enjoyed their company, especially noting Monyetta's impressive demeanor, which left a lasting impression on him. Von was totally convinced of her authenticity from that day forward. With his grandfather's endorsement, Von began to prioritize their relationship more, wondering just how deep could their love go.

Once the youngsters left Hound's home, hey headed to Atlantic City for a bit of fun at the gambling tables and slot machines. Von treated them. They had a great time together, enjoying the night until the early hours. The girls checked into the suite early, while Von was restless and kept busy moving around, networking and making connections. Kidada sensed something intriguing about Monyetta and felt a compelling urge to explore further. And so, this was what she'd made it her business to do.

Chapter 3

Four Months Later . . .
The relationship between Lily and Jamar grew stronger, forming a seemingly unbreakable bond. This followed her release from jail awaiting trial. Despite the challenges, the two stayed together, often spending hours at her place. Jamar harbored immense love and respect for Lily, desiring a long-term and committed relationship with her. However, Lily didn't share that same desire, particularly when it came to having more children. Trevon was enough for her. He was her one and only.

When it came to a long-term commitment, Lily didn't prioritize this either. The uncertainty of her legal ordeal fueled a change of heart, especially with Von's father soon to return home in free society. Hound Jr. hinted at his interest, leaving her unsure of his intentions—whether to rekindle their past or establish a business connection. She anticipated her son's father would want to reconnect in some capacity. Above all, she was determined not to miss the chance to be the first person Little Hound came home to, rather than Kidada's mother, Juanita.

Lily and Jamar were at his place on this night. She was intent on reiterating her decision to end things at the particular time. *This was for the best*, Lily believed. With resolve, she proceeded to inform Jamar that her decision was final. They needed to part ways.

"Lily, what seems to be bothering you today, baby?" Jamar asked her. They were seated on the bed in sleepwear. It was night time, around 12 A.M.

"Been having a lot on my mind lately. So many tough decisions that's needed to be made," Lily responded.

"Is that so? You care to talk about anything to help clear your mind?"

"To be honest Jamar, I have no choice *but* to talk with you about one of the main issues I have on the mind. It concerns you and I."

"Issues!" Jamar retorted. "This don't sound good. But go ahead anyway. Let's get on with it."

"I wouldn't necessarily say this is anything of an issue. Maybe I used the wrong term—"

"Go ahead and speak your peace, Lily. You know I'm the type of man who doesn't like for people to beat around the bush." Jamar urged her to say what she needed to say.

"We can't continue to do this any longer, Jamar. My son's father is on his way home soon. And I have to give him the level of respect that was in place before he got locked up," Lily reluctantly said.

Jamar was completely taken aback by her words. He was at a temporary uncertainty of how to respond. There had to be something he could say in return. Undoubtedly, his feelings were caught up in her, but not to the point where he couldn't maintain control of his emotions.

"Are you serious, Lily! Really?" Jamar said in a mild, non-threatening tone of voice.

She shook head in disgust about the occasion.

"I do love you, Jamar. And yes, I want us to remain friends as we are. Is this something you would consider? However, Cornelius and I have too much invested, and too much in each other to let it all go. I didn't anticipate him being freed early. Nonetheless, he is."

"What about us, Lily? Everything you've said? All the promises you've made? The future you claim to have? So... what . . . were you just *gas-lighting* me or something?"

"Jamar. I don't even plan on losing you from my life forever, sweetheart. The relationship I have with my son's father is more about business and what I know of his life and that of his family more than anything else. To be blunt, I know where the money is stashed, and, I know where the bodies are buried. Cornelius was a dedicated street dude, Jamar. I don't want any conflict to develop between you and him. So let's just call it quits while we're ahead, and see one each other when we get the chance, okay?" Lily properly put things into perspective. "And just so you know, he was the one who told me to go and live my life. That he knew I had wants and needs that require attention by a man, physically, mentally, and spiritually. He wasn't able to fulfill those needs, and didn't want to slow me down in any way," Lily further stated.

"It ain't no thing, Lily. I understand. And I don't have any problem with any of it either, so long as I do get to see you and have the chance to hit this pussy you got on you when it's my turn to," said Jamar, as he hugged Lily tightly and kissed on her neck.

"You know you're gonna always be an important person in my life, Jamar. This isn't the end. Only for a time being."

"So I don't have to worry about this being farewell sex then, do I?"

Lily locked eyes with him and cooed with sensation. "Nah. You don't have to worry about that. We're gonna always be accessible in that area. Always!" Lily declared.

They then began to tongue-kiss as they indulged within the stimulating act of foreplay. Once naked again, the sex took them well into the wee hours. Lily felt the need to put it on Jamar the way she had, because there wasn't no telling when the next time would be for them to hook up for more of the same. Little Hound was on his way home. She didn't know when. All she knew was *soon*. And Lily knew she had to be on her best behavior. She had no problem doing so for him. Little Hound's leadership and management capabilities was what Lily hungered for. She was drunk in love with that particular Savage. Cornelius Savage II.

Chapter 4

Three Months Later...

The pivotal moment had arrived for Von's father, Little Hound. He'd managed to have his convictions and sentence overturned and had his lawyer consult with the U.S. Attorney's office for a term of time served and only one year under supervised release. The day of freedom was finally upon him.

It was the first Monday of September 2009. Hound Jr emerged from the federal prison facility in Coleman, Florida. Drip and the attorney, Levi Jacobson, picked him up at the front gate. Together, they embarked on their journey to Tampa where a private jet awaited to whisk them back to Philly.

Once back in the city of 'Brotherly Love," Hound Jr thanked Levi for his assistance throughout the year before Levi took his leave from his case, pleased that he had served yet another client well. Hound Jr and Drip then entered the Range Rover where Body awaited behind the wheel. The tension between Hound Jr and Body was palpable; their relationship had already seen its share of disappointments and failures prior to, for whatever their reasons were. Nevertheless, Body greeted Hound Jr. And desired to reconcile those differences of the past.

"What's good, homie?" Body said. "Long time."

"Oh shit! What up, Body? How have you been, bro?" Hound Jr responded, keeping his true feelings of the man in check.

"I just been coolin' man. Me and Drip doing what we do, and keeping business top priority. I'm glad to see you. We're on a whole different level now, player. You'll see."

"I'm glad to be home and I'm ready to make business a top priority along with y'all. It's been long enough. And now the time has come. Eleven years in the pen. But I'm back now, baby. One of your beloved sons has made it home, Philly!" Hound Jr shouted in excitement.

"I know that's right. But wait until you see what I've got in stow for you, man. You're gonna make your way back to the top in no time, fam," Drip stated. He had a solid plan in place to ensure his favorite cousin succeeded.

"No doubt. And I'm ready to get to it. I've been preparing for a long time now. I'm ready to see my kids and family as well," Hound Jr responded.

Body began to drive from that point; they were on their way to Drip's penthouse suite. From there, they would head to the home of Big Hound for Hound Jr to reconnect with his parents and other family members. Drip had a surprise for his cousin once they made it to the second home he owned.

****

They'd made it to century-city Philly. Body pulled into the parking lobby of the building.

"Damn, fam!" Hound Jr exclaimed. "You did say you was doing it big, didn't you? I ain't know you were doing it this *big*. A fucking penthouse, in downtown Philly! Oh yeah, you are on your 'A-Game.' Now . . . I gotta get my shit together and build up to this point. You really living. And that's saying a lot, fam."

"You ain't seen nothing yet. Wait until you see the one I got over in Norristown. And all you gotta do is have some patience, and continue to let me lead the way, fam. My people go as I go. Ain't no Savage or close homie of mine left behind, you feel me?" Drip stated confidently.

"I know that's right!" Hound Jr responded.

The trio got out the S.U.V. and made their way to the lobby. They got on the elevator and arrived at Drip's front door. He used the key card to open the door.

"Welcome to my place, fam! Drip's playboy lounge!" he said with both arms spread wide and gesturing for Hound Jr to enjoy the view.

"Drip's playboy lounge, huh? I like that, and what about the surprise you say you got for me?"

"I got that too," he declared. Drip then yelled out loud enough for the guests to hear him. "Y'all come on out!"

Three sexy females came from the back. Amongst them was Drip's young college sweetheart, Divida. She was accompanied by her twin sister–Daniella, and Divida's friend, Porsche. Daniella was there for Hound Jr, while Porsche was Body's date. They'd already began what they had. The girls were there already hiding out. Drip had texted them once they'd left the airport.

"Ooh shit! What do we have here? My God!" Hound Jr said with a smile. "All three for me?"

"Nah, fam!" Drip let out with a hard chuckle. "The one in the middle is for you. The other two for me and the homie, Body!" Drip replied, still smiling joyously.

All three of the ladies were wearing heels and colorful two-piece outfits. Daniella then seductively sashayed up to Hound Jr. She smiled and introduced herself.

"Hi! I'm Daniella. I've heard so many nice things about you. I couldn't wait to meet you. And you look very nice," she said. "Healthy even."

"It's nice to meet you too, Daniella. You sexy as hell, sweetheart! I've been locked up for a while, as you may know. You sure you gonna be able to tame this wild beast in bed? I might be too much for you, boo. And why you two look alike? Y'all twins or something?" Hound Jr stated in a humorous way.

"Yes. We are. And I'd rather you be too much for me as a man than too less for me as one. That way, I'll still have room to grow and be the type of woman you would want me to be for you," Daniella responded.

"That's one hell of a comeback, babe. I like you already," the OG Savage said to her. They then hugged and began to kiss.

Hound Jr. ran his hands up and down the body and over the booty of Daniella. She wanted him to go all the way with her. The other four looked on at them and smiled at the way the two connected.

"Say, fam, I bought you a full wardrobe of clothes too. I've got them in my bedroom. But in the meantime, welcome home. Enjoy yourself!" Drip said. He then hit a button on one of the remotes, and the surround sound came on. The music began to play at a modest level. "And Kiki was the one who gave me your sizes too. So you'd know."

"Fam, I wanna shower and get fresh," Hound Jr. said to Drip.

"No doubt. Daniella gonna show you where the bathroom at."

Daniella continued to look on at Hound Jr, then gently grabbed him by the hand to lead him towards the direction of the wash room.

"I ain't got no problem with that. You showering with me too, beautiful? I hope so."

"I'm all yours, sweetheart. I do all you want me to do," the young pretty heartthrob replied.

Drip and Body began to unwind and relax themselves. The time was only 2 P.M. They took a seat on the sectional. Divida and Porsche made drinks of champagne and wine for them while Hound Jr and Daniella were in the shower. More than likely they were fucking all the while. It was a beautiful affair.

****

Four Hours Later . . .

Hound Jr had himself a good time banging Daniella out in the shower and the bedroom. He'd dressed, and was now on the way to his father's house, accompanied by Drip and Body.

They'd made it to the Brookfield Terrace gated community just on the outside of Southwest Philly. Once at the home, they got out and approached the front door. Hound Jr rang the doorbell. Big Hound's wife answered.

"Who is it?" she asked.

"Momma Henrietta. It's me, Junior," he responded.

She recognized the voice, took a look through the peephole to know who exactly it was, then proceeded to open the door.

"It is you, ain't it, Junior! How you doing, baby?" the elderly lady said with excitement.

"Yeah, it's me, momma. They let me out today."

The step-mother and step-son then hugged tightly. She kissed him on the cheek bone.

"Where Daddy?"

Big Hound was in his favorite area of the house, the den.

"Your father hasn't changed too much, son. You know where he's at!" Henrietta replied with a smile. He's gonna be so happy having you back home. Everyone will be."

"Hey, auntie. How you doing?" Drip spoke to her.

"Hey, Damien. Haven't seen you in a while. You been okay?"

"Yes, ma'am. I have. This is my friend here. Actually *our* friend," Drip said, referring to himself and Hound Jr. "His name, Bruce."

"Hello, Bruce, welcome to my home."

"Nice to meet you, ma'am. You have a beautiful place," Body responded.

The four then made steps towards the den. Hound Jr led the way. He knew the house well.

He reached the entrance of the room.

"Pops! I'm home! I made it!" Hound Jr said energetically.

Big Hound turned his head away from the TV momentarily to have a look at who was there. He couldn't believe his eyes. "Junior! Hey! How you doing, son? You made it home, didn't you! Come here, boy, and give me a hug," the father said as he got to his feet and hugged his first born tightly. He kissed him on the forehead as well.

"I got out this morning, pop. Damien made everything happen for me."

"Well, ain't that something? You're a good man, Damien," Hound Sr. turned and said to Drip. "How Mickey been doing? I hope to see him and Johnny Mack again sometime soon."

Mickey Savage was the grandfather of Drip and the first cousin of Hound Sr. Johnny Mack was the first cousin of Hound Sr. and Mickey, and he was also the eldest of the three. Those three OG's were the sons of three brothers and originally born and raised in Savannah, Georgia. Hound Sr., Mickey, and Johnny Mack made their way to Philly in the year 1958. Tragic reasons forced them to the north. A couple of white police officers had been shot and killed during an illegal search of a home.

Drip spoke once more. "Yeah. Grandpa Mickey doing good, he and grandma JoJo. You know they be back and forth between Philly and New Hampshire. More than likely, they'll be back in time for me to take y'all to the 'Kentucky Derby,' the 'Preakness,' and the 'Belmont Stakes' horse races y'all love so much. We missed it this past year, but we won't miss it next time," Drip assured. The old-timers loved horse and dog races for placing bets. This was an obsession.

"I can't wait, Damien. You know the races and baseball are our favorite pastimes. But anyway, who else know you home, Junior?"

"Nobody, Pop. I'm about to make calls and let everybody know now."

"I can call Vonnie and Lily now, fam," Drip said. He then dialed Von's number.

Hound Jr. knew Kidada's number by heart. He called her from the house phone. She was excited as ever to know her father had made it home. Her leg work and errands for him had something to do with his release as well. She'd quickly got up and began the drive from her mother's house to her grandpop's.

Von himself had already been in Philly throughout the time he was away from Williamsport. He was relaxing at Monyetta's apartment prior to getting a call and the both of them making their way to his granddad's house, joined by Lily as well.

* * * *

One Hour Later . . .

Von, Monyetta, Lily, and Kidada all arrived at Hound Sr.'s house, thrilled that Hound Jr was home from prison. Everyone gathered in the den and engaged in lively conversation. Hound Sr. and his son then made a move to the backroom for a private discussion. Big Hound led the way to the side of the house. He held money for his son in a special location there.

"Well, Junior. I don't have all your money here on me. Only a half million, the rest in the bank. I know you ready to buy you a car and get your life back on track. Welcome home, son. I love you and I'm glad you're free. I'm just happy I'm still alive to see this day come to pass. God is good," Hound Sr. said.

"I'm glad to be home too, Pop. And I'm glad you're still here to be with me on my first day of freedom. Now I've gotta be sure Lily still got all my money I had her to keep for me. Let me get her and Vonnie in here for a moment. Kidada too."

He then stepped back in the den area to have his son, daughter, and ex-girlfriend join him and his father. They couldn't stop smiling and being enamored at one another. The private conversation between them began.

"What's the situation with you, Vonnie?" Hound Jr. asked.

"They still want me, Pop."

"Who wants you, son?" Hound Sr. asked of Von. The old-timer had no clue what was going on.

"The cops, grandpop. I've got myself in a situation."

"How I don't know about this, Son?"

"I was gonna mention it to you, grandpa. But I didn't want to upset you any type of way."

"Why didn't I know about this, bro?" Kidada asked.

"We're gonna be sure to work it out at some point soon. Even if I've gotta just turn myself in."

"And you, Lily?" Hound Jr asked.

"Of course you know I'm out on bail. My first court appearance isn't until February next year coming up."

"Would you and Vonnie please tell me what the hell happened that day? Me and Pop need to know so we can offer help and advice. And that money of mine you got, Lily—"

"Everything is still in place, Cornelius. And I've got some of it in the bank," Lily clarified.

"Okay. Good. But I need to know the story of what happened."

Both Lily and Von explained the events that took place the day Von shot and killed Bernard.

Hound Sr. had a thing or two to say on that.

"Vonnie, that sounds like a case of self-defense *or* justifiable homicide to me. Why didn't you just wait for the cops to come, and explain, then call me? I actually had a working relationship with the grandfather and father of the

Assistant District Attorney in office now. He has a lot of influence over his boss, the head D.A. I've done business with the Marconis for decades, son."

"I panicked, grandpop. I didn't know what to do."

"And your mom had to go to jail all those days to protect you, when y'all could have resolved the issue with one phone call," Hound Sr. stated.

"I had too much going on, grandpop. I couldn't go to jail," Von said.

"Too much going on! Where, in school?" the grandfather uttered.

Von definitely had to now explain.

"I made a decision in my life, grandpa. I wanted to be like you and my dad. I got involved in the streets. I became a hustler. I sell dope now. And I'm making a lot of money while I'm at it. Not to mention, I got three babies on the way at one time."

"Three babies! Vonnie! What the hell!" Lily exclaimed. Apparently, she heard not a word about Von confessing to being a heavy dope dealer. Those words weren't captured.

Von simply looked on at his mother and everyone else present.

"You got a lot going on, son. A whole lot!" Hound Jr stated.

"You certainly do," said Hound Sr. "But we can deal with all that another day. Right now, let's just celebrate Junior being home, and show him some love, shall we!"

Kidada looked on at her brother and smiled while shaking her head. He'd taken her by surprise with the 'three babies' revelation. At no time had Monyetta said anything to her about being pregnant. Now, she knew without a doubt that he had three side chicks carrying his seed. Von had no self-control sexually.

"Vonnie, me and you gonna have to have a talk, a'ight?" Kidada stated.

Von nodded to indicate *yes* to his sister. He pitied himself for being a disappointment. At no time did he desire to be this towards them.

The five continued to discuss the future, then, rejoined the others in the den. They enjoyed food, had drinks, and reveled in Hound Jr's homecoming. Drip and Body then left. Hound Jr wanted to spend his first day free at his father's house. There was a lot of conversation he wanted to have with everyone still present, especially with his son, Vonnie. The two had so much to be discussed.

Chapter 5

The Next Day . . .

Hound Jr awoke bright and early. He was filled with eagerness to begin his day. He had a series of errands to attend to. First and foremost, a visit to the Federal Probation Office awaited him, marking the beginning of his one-year supervised release. Following that, a trip to the DMV was in order. Additionally, he planned to stop by the Apple store to acquire a phone, a laptop, and other necessary devices. And also, accompanying Lily to deliver the money to him she had retained was on his agenda, although she seemed to have different intentions. Unaware that he viewed their relationship solely as a friendship, she harbored romantic aspirations. However, Hound Jr's attention was captivated by another. A young lady, whose company made him feel youthful once more. Their connection was undeniable, and their intimacy was fulfilling in every aspect. Not to mention, she was the first to put the pussy on him moments after his freedom was restored, and he felt compelled to have her ahead of everyone else. This was Daniella.

Little Hound had asked Kidada to pick him up. The both of them were to spend the day together. "Damn, pop! You're fresh to death, ain't you!" Kidada said, admiring the outfit her father had on.

He loved to style and dress in designer sportswear. In fact, Hound Jr was the one Drip got his swag from. His outfit for the day consisted of a Bally sweat suit, complete with matching sneakers, hat, and undershirt, in black and red colors.

"You like this?" he responded.

"Hell yeah, I do. You look real dapper. Like you're twenty all over again. What young *jawn* you met that's got you looking to appeal to her?"

Little Hound looked at his daughter and smiled. He surmised that Daniella was only one year older than Kidada, and felt the need to know how she would feel to know he dated someone her age or just above it?

"Well, when you're my age, and you got a twenty-year-old college sweetheart in your life, you have to look and act the part."

"You got it like that, huh? Where you two meet?"

"We hooked up yesterday. Her name is Daniella and she's the twin sister of Drip's girl. He had her there at his place as a surprise for me. And damn, she's nice, baby. We had a good time," Hound Jr said with a loving smile and a capacity for having vigorous energy.

"Mmm-hmm, pop, I bet you did," Kidada responded with a loving smile of her own. She was happy to know that her father was still able to attract a pretty young lady and that he was happy.

"You know your pop gonna keep it all the way real with you. I know no other way. And it makes me proud to know you and I have this type of relationship, baby. I don't hold nothing back from you, we keep no secrets. You're the only one I don't hold nothing back from. I can't say that about my other two, Vonnie, and Aaron. But you—You're my A-one, Kiki. And daddy love you!" Hound Jr said while hugging his daughter and kissing her on the forehead.

"I love you too, O.G. And I wanna meet this *Daniella* . . . today, too. A'ight."

"No problem. I was gonna do that anyway. I might need y'all to form a friendship. I'm looking to make power moves in the near future."

"That's a bet. Vonnie did the same thing with me and his girl Monyetta. And now, me and her are really close. Not a day goes by that we don't talk. I really fuck with Monyetta. She's my type of bitch. Even if her and Vonnie don't work out, me and her are still gonna be good."

"She is nice, ain't she? And how the hell Vonnie got himself three babies on the way, at the same damn time? That boy got too much going on!" Hound Jr said while shaking his head in disbelief.

"He did trip out with that, didn't he?" Kidada remarked.

"Damn sure did. We definitely gotta talk," the father replied.

"I just hope he get his legal situation together first, before the first baby of his is born. From my understanding, the due dates are next month and November."

"Does Monyetta know anything about the three side-pieces being pregnant?" Hound Jr. asked.

"Not that I know of. More than likely, she don't. She would've mentioned it to me by now. Or at least wanted to have a conversation about it."

"He's gonna have to bring it to her attention at some point soon. But obviously, he knows what he's doing and what he gotta do. He just gotta man up about everything. That's all there is to it."

"That's all he's gotta do, Pop. Keep it real with them," Kidada responded.

She continued to chat with her father further while steering the 3-series BMW she owned in the direction of the Federal building downtown. Following the visit there, Kidada would head to the Apple store on Market Street not far away.

Hound was arrested long before the debut of the *iPhone*, and no doubt, he'd seen and heard so much about them on TV, that he definitely wanted one. Through phone conversations he had with Vonnie about the devices, he couldn't control his desire to own more than one item by the

Apple brand. Finally, the opportunity had arrived. And he was looking to capitalize on it.

They went to the DMV from there. With his license reinstated, Hound Jr. was now legally able to drive again. He took the wheel of Kidada's car right then and there. She looked at him and smiled in delight from the passenger seat.

The father and daughter then made stops at other locations which they needed to visit. Lily had to work, and wouldn't be off until later in the day. Hound Jr would then get his money from her at that time. But in between, he was ready to introduce Kidada and Daniella to one another. He logged in to his Messenger account to get her phone number and then called.

After completing the call, he contacted Drip, who was at the newly renovated *Ozone Bar and Grill* he owned, preparing for the upcoming grand opening that Friday. Drip told him to stop by. The location of the bar on 6th and Spring Garden wasn't too far from where they were. Hound Jr. simply took the one-way 7th Street North to get there. He and Kidada were now on site. They entered.

"What's good, fam? How is you and Kiki?" Drip greeted.

"Oh shit! Lil Hound! How you doing, fam?" Monk greeted Hound as well. He was there assisting his brother. "You and Lil Cuz, Kiki?" They all took turns embracing one another.

"Ol' Monk. You done grown up, ain't you. I'm glad to see you, young boul. I really am!" Hound Jr stated.

"Me too, Monk. I ain't seen you in a minute," Kidada chimed in to say. "And Drip, what you got going on here, fam! This a nice spot."

"Yeah, this my new business here. Opening Friday night. As always, you're invited. Family is always welcomed. Be sure to be here. We're gonna have a welcome home party for your Pop. This place gonna be lit. Like for real, it is!" Drip responded with much confidence.

"I got a question. Daniella know how to get here?" Hound Jr asked of Drip.

"I don't know. Maybe Vida mentioned something to her about this spot before. Maybe not. Text her to let her know how to get here. And I see y'all two got it going on already. That's a good thing, fam."

"I know that's right," Hound Jr responded. He then proceeded to text Daniella to let her know where he would like for her to meet him.

"Come on to my office, fam. Let us enjoy a few drinks together," Drip said.

Everyone then went to the bar to place an order of what they wanted to drink. Drip had a cute fine-ass bartender named Raven doing the serving; she was the bar supervisor. Raven was an ebony dime-piece, no doubt.

They then made their way up the stairs to the third floor where the office suites were. Raven would later deliver the drinks once they'd been prepared.

Drip's office space had undergone a luxurious transformation. It was equipped with state-of-the-art appliances and top-notch accommodations. The surround sound system played throughout the building, with the track, *This Is The Life,* by rapper *Rick Ross* resonating through the speakers. Monk sang along to the lyrics in a low tone of voice as the four family members lounged inside the suite and carried on a meaningful conversation.

"I'm sure this is where you spend most of your time now, huh, fam? I can do this all day. If I had your pockets!" Hound Jr stated. "And once again, I like that nice ass penthouse you got too, Drip."

"For the most part, yeah. This is where I'm at. I like being in the midst of things and part of the action. *The Ozone* is gonna give me the opportunity to do so. And now it's football season, I'm most definitely gonna be preoccupied here most days. Hell, who knows, I might get somebody down here to start booking parlay and pool tickets to pass to the experience," Drip responded. "And be patient, fam. You're home now. My family is gonna do all that I do . . . be all that I am . . . and eat the same way that I eat. Ain't no doubt about that."

"Well, I've got my license situated again. Gotta get a ride now," Hound Jr made Drip aware.

"What type of whip you got in mind?"

"I like the way that Range Rover you got floated on the road. I may get one of them. I don't want a car. I want an SUV this time around."

"That's a good choice. I fell in love with the Range myself when I first drove one."

"I love my cars," Monk chimed in. "My Benz is the perfect fit for me."

"You made your mind up yet where you gonna be staying?" Drip asked.

"Shit I'mma be here and there for the time being, until I get my own place. You know I've got to get me a spot outside the city somewhere," Hound Jr responded.

The casual conversation went on.

Not too long afterwards, Daniella showed up. Her and her twin. They made their way up the stairs to the office. Hound Jr immediately got to his feet and walked up to Daniella. He gave her a hug and a tongue-kiss. The two were so happy to see each other for a second time.

Drip and Divida did the same.

"I want you to meet somebody, Daniella. This is Kidada, my daughter. And I've already told her about you. So no pressure," Hound Jr introduced.

"Hello, Kidada! Nice to meet you. I'm Daniella."

"Nice to meet you too, Daniella. And yes, my dad has mentioned much to me about you. Just be sure to keep it real with him. If you don't do nothing else. Keep it real. Stay true to who you are and be upright," Kidada said to the brown-skinned exotic cutie. She had a level of seriousness to her voice to clearly indicate how for real she was about her ol' man.

Daniella returned the same degree of eye contact towards Kidada, and nodded.

"Trust and believe me, I keep it real at all times. With myself and others. And your dad is the type of OG I truly desire to have and experience life with. But, of course, we have to continue getting to know one another first. Something that I'm willing to do."

"Point taken. But enough with that. You have a unique dress code. I like your style. What labels are those?" Kidada asked.

"This is Chanel. My favorite brand. I love to shop. Me and my sister!" Daniella said. She and Divida made eye contact and smiled at each other at her utterance.

"I'm hoping the three of us can go on shopping sprees together whenever our time allows," Divida said to Kidada.

"Indeed. My father is home now. So I know I don't have to worry about anything," Kidada stated

"Sure don't" Hound Jr said, then kissed his daughter on the forehead and hugged her.

The group then continued to talk, lounged around, and enjoyed their drinks.

Before Hound Jr. and Kidada left, he and Daniella made plans to meet up later in the day. He wanted to reserve a hotel suite at one of the ritziest spots downtown Philly. It was clear that they were into each other.

****

Hound Jr had Kidada take him to a luxury car rental. He'd chosen a black Range Rover to get around in. True to his promise to Drip about appreciating the ride of this style of SUV, he wanted to familiarize himself with the brand as soon as possible. And this he'd done.

Lily texted him, directing him to meet her at her mother's home in Germantown. Although Hound Jr. and Mrs. Edna were not well-acquainted any longer, he managed to make his way to her place and waited for Lily to arrive. During his conversation with Mrs. Edna, they discussed various topics, including his son's problems and the raid on her house, as well as the mistreatment of her by the police. Hound Jr still didn't know or understand why Lily wanted to meet him at her mother's home, and not at the home they'd bought together. Nevertheless, he had no problem spending a little time with Mrs. Edna.

Finally, Lily arrived. She and Hound Jr began their conversation immediately. She couldn't stop smiling at the sight of him free again. "I see you making progress in the free world with no problems," she said, referring to the rental and what she knew of Daniella.

"Ah yeah, I had Kiki rent that for me today when we left the DMV. I may buy me one next month. Maybe next week, if I continue to fall in love with it."

"And you're gonna be staying where?"

"I'll be at my dad's and Kiki's place for the most part. Until I figure out where I wanna get a place to live on my own,"

"What about our house we own together?"

"I let you have that house, Lily. Remember? That's the reason why I didn't never put my name on the deed. I got locked up and went away on you and our son. The least I could've done was to leave you with a roof over y'all head and money to keep the bills paid. And that, I did. So you go on and continue to keep the place for yourself. I'mma start all the way over. It's a new beginning for me. A brand new beginning."

"So just forget all about the me and what I want to have, huh?" Lily said.

"I didn't say that. What I will say is that, I want us to be friends and cool. Like we are now. Just continue to do what you do, and I'mma continue to do what I do. Ain't no need to rush into nothing. But look. That money you're holding for me. I need it," Hound Jr. said.

Lily got to her feet, went to the back of the house, and returned maybe two minutes later with mini duffle bag loaded with cash. She'd gotten everything together for him the night before returning from Big Hound's house. She handed it to him.

"Here you go. It's all there. I hope you do the right thing with it, Cornelius," Lily said.

He accepted the bag from her and opened to have a look at the contents inside. His eyes widened. Dude hadn't seen that type of cash since he'd gotten locked up.

"Now about this 'friends and being cool' scenario. Do we at least include fucking and foreplay into the equation?" Lily stated, then eased open her blouse to expose those caramel colored luscious set of titties she had.

"Yeah, we do. But remember. After this, I've got a few things I want you to know. A'ight."

"Okay. Now come on, and give me what I've been waiting eleven years to get. I miss it too," Lily let out.

Hound Jr. stood to his feet. He and Lily then made their way to the back room of the house so her mother wouldn't hear them panting and exhaling in sexual pleasure, if they were to get into all of the above.

Truth be told, Hound Jr didn't really have an interest in Lily sexually. He had Daniella on his mind. But was willing to give into Lily for oral sex. She had no issue with giving him a blow job. So long as she got some type of action out of him. This was fine by her. Very fine by her.

Chapter 6

Cold Heart and his new sweetheart—Tiona—did spend plenty of time together and were always busy building a strong relationship. He stayed at her place most nights, and their bond was solidifying. Especially regarding the bright future that they had in mind to build and explore together. For the upcoming weekend, he wanted to draw attention to the fact that they'd been invited to a bar opening— *The Ozone*—where Drip wanted both of them to be present.

"Yo, Tee. You not gonna be too busy with anything this Friday, are you? We got invited to the grand opening of my homie's bar. It's gonna also be the home-coming party for Von's dad too. He got out Monday. It's the Ozone bar and grill down on Spring Garden," he said

"Nah, boo. I don't have too much of nothing going on. My sister already mentioned something to me about the grand opening. We wanted to go shopping for outfits to wear," Tiona responded.

"Okay, good. We definitely gotta step out in style to show support for my two homies. How much do you need?"

"Whatever you feel like I should have, babe."

Cold Heart went into the closet; he had a few thousand dollars stashed at the spot in a small safe. He gave her $3,500. Tiona already knew to buy him something from the money. She planned to purchase him a pair of slacks, a button-down shirt, a vest, bow-tie, and a hat, as well as a pair of wingtip shoes.

"Here you go," Cold Heart said, then gave her the money and a kiss. "Now I've gotta get outta here. Got some business to take care of."

"Okay, baby. Have a nice day. I'll call you if I need to."

Cold Heart then left her bedroom, walked out the front door, and got into his car. He was headed up to Williamsport to meet with Von and the rest of the crew already assembled there. Drip's Mexican suppliers were back, and they had product ready for distribution. In particular, Drip wanted this line of product sold in the upstate locales. Monk also was already in place to ensure that the operation progressed smoothly. Failure wasn't an option.

Chapter 7

The Friday evening Drip long awaited, which marked the grand opening of *the Ozone*, was upon him. This was a milestone in his property development and real estate career. It was a place he had had a hand in on from the very beginning . . . from concept to the day that had arrived. And now, he felt immensely proud of himself. *The Ozone* could become his daily hangout spot like he anticipated it to be; his most celebrated business venture.

The second week of the College Football Season was in effect, and also, it was Week 1 of the NFL Football season to kick off simultaneously. *The Ozone* would serve as a haven for sports fans to enjoy the games and socialize how they saw fit.

All the invited guests showed up. There was Monk and Ayonna... Divida and Daniella... Von and Monyetta... Cold Heart and Tiona... as well as Hound Jr. and Lily. For sure, Hound Jr. had taken it upon himself to properly explain to Daniella what the nature of his relationship with Lily was all about. He wanted to ensure that there were no misunderstandings or misconceptions about their connection. Hound Jr. emphasized that he and Lily shared deep history, a son, and a friendship, but nothing more. Daniella respected his honesty and openness about it and didn't give him any trouble regarding.

Might it also be mentioned, Kidada was also present as well. She had a male friend tag along with her. He was a gay guy, known by the moniker 'Passion Fruit' or simply 'Passion.' Adrian Cooper was his given name.

Kidada didn't prioritize having a boyfriend, though she did have one with whom she occasionally spent time. Her preference leaned more so towards her female companions. The bisexual appetite she possessed couldn't be so easily satiated. Besides, she cherished the intimate and exclusive bond she now shared with Monyetta, of all people. But her and the brother couldn't both have her. Or could they?

****

Amidst the gathering, a lurking figure awaited. He was poised to strike. He harbored intentions to carry out a hit. His loaded gun snug against his waistline. Bullets bearing specific names.

Unbeknownst to Drip, a grave oversight had occurred. Metal detectors were absent at the entrance, and security personnel lacked wands to check for weapons. No consideration was given to the potential eruption of chaos, as is often the case.

As Drip, Monk, Von, Cold Heart, Hound Jr, Kidada, other members of the Savage family, and even Lily, gathered in the photo-taking section, the assailant wormed his way through the crowd towards his target, inching ever so closer with intent. The area stood adjacent to the front door, flanked by a large glass window.

While they were standing, smiling, holding expensive bottles of champagne and cigars, and flashing large wads of cash, the ill-intended man seized the moment to take aim.

Bang!

The first round echoed through the air. Chaos erupted as the crowd scattered in all directions, desperate to evade becoming casualties in the unfolding turmoil.

Bang!

Another shot pierced the air. The overhead light was deliberately shattered, plunging the first level into sparse illumination.

Bang-Bang-Bang-Bang-Bang!

Five more shots followed suit. Three people fell victim to the assailant's gunfire, as he brazenly initiated his escape. Darting through the crowd like a frantic running back, he collided with bystanders, leaving chaos in his wake. It became evident that he was the shooter, prompting security to pursue him vehemently.

Bang!

Another shot resounded, deterring the security personnel from closing in. The crowd's exit pace failed to satisfy the increasingly agitated gunman.

Seizing one of the nearby waitresses who was clad in a two-piece outfit—a somewhat slim and agile female—the assailant tossed her over his left shoulder (despite being left-handed). Brandishing the Glock .40 pistol with his left hand, he gestured menacingly from side to side, compelling bystanders to clear a path or face the threat of gunfire. With the waitress in tow, he sprinted toward the expansive glass window, firing multiple shots with his right hand that weakened its structure and pockmarked its surface. With a final burst of force, he hurled himself and the waitress through the window. Their combined momentum caused the glass to shatter effortlessly, and they landed on the concrete on the opposite side with a controlled roll to minimize injury.

The shooter scrambled to his feet, his head whipping from left to right in a frantic search to ensure no one was attempting to apprehend him. With a sense of urgency, he bolted down the street towards an awaiting getaway car.

****

Inside *the Ozone*, people began to assess themselves to determine if or not they'd been hit. When the shots rang out, most of those capturing pictures instinctively leaped into action to shield and protect Drip. Fortunately, he escaped unscathed. However, Ayonna, Lily, and *Von* (of all people) were not as fortunate—they had sustained injuries, with Von's being the most severe. He was in critical condition, bleeding out heavily, and drifting in and out of consciousness. Immediate medical attention was imperative. If not, he'd surely die.

Chapter 8

Ayonna sustained a gunshot wound to her inner left thigh, Lily, one to the gut and right arm, and Vonnie, took one to the gut and another to the chest. All three victims were on laid out on the floor, receiving urgent attention from those around them. Quick-thinking individuals wrapped their wounds to staunch the bleeding. As Von's condition became apparent, the urgency to take him to the hospital grew. Recognizing the severity of his injuries, Hound Jr, Cold Heart, Drip, Monk, and a few others swiftly carried Von out the door and placed him in Drip's Range Rover parked directly out front. They raced to Temple University Hospital, knowing that time was of the essence. Lily and Ayonna were placed into Monk's car and transported to the same destination

The authorities were notified, and they promptly responded to *the Ozone*. Upon the arrival of the three gunshot victims at the medical center, police protocol mandated notification. Another team of investigators arrived at the hospital to assess the victims and potentially question them. Von was rushed into the emergency room for immediate surgery, whereas the other two didn't have life-threatening injuries.

The medical staff attending to Lily found it increasingly challenging as she remained in a state of hysteria, consumed by panic over her son's injury and potential mortality. Despite her own wounds, she was solely focused on his well-being. The bullet that pierced her gut had merely passed through cleanly. The doctor administering her treatment decided to administer medication through an IV to sedate and soothe her, aiming to calm her without rendering her unconscious.

"Is my son okay? Please tell me he's not dead! How is my son doing?" Lily asked.

"Ma'am, the male who was also shot, was immediately taken into the emergency room to have surgery. We don't have an update on his status at this time. Who is he? May we have a name? Yours as well?" the senior female medical staff member asked.

"I'm Lillian Dietrich, ma'am. And my son's name is Trevon Savage. Please don't let my son die! Please don't!"

The nurse wrote down the name provided on a notepad.

"Ma'am, rest assured, we're committed to providing the best medical care possible to you, your son, and the other young lady, okay?"

"Please do. Don't let my son die. That's all I ask. That is all I ask," Lily pleaded, her voice steady as tears streamed down her face, mixing with her prayers.

Von's situation was dire.

****

Back at *the Ozone*, Body and the other two security personnel on hand managed to quell the chaos and regain control of the situation. Almost everyone had departed, leaving only a handful behind. Remaining were Kidada and her friend, the twins Divida and Daniella, a few other Savage family members along with a couple of patrons who'd attended the event.

Tears welled in Kidada's eyes. Her emotion leaned more towards sorrow than anger, yet she was determined to take action and seek retribution against those responsible.

"I'm still trying to process what the fuck happened, y'all!" she said to the twins and her people. "Did anybody get a look at what the shooter looked like?"

"I don't think nobody did. It happened so fast, you know," Divida responded.

The truth was, nobody knew who had done it or why. Drip had security cameras installed and would likely review the footage to try and identify the shooter. Kidada and everyone close to him had witnessed Von lying on the floor. It was a harrowing sight. Blood was everywhere, painting a grim picture. Adding to the chaos, the venue had sustained further damage as the panicked crowd scrambled towards the exit, toppling tables, chairs, and other objects in their path.

Drip made it his business to call Body, instructing him to shut down the bar and secure the doors until he returned. He promised to do so soon, so to pick him up. It was now war; somebody had flagrantly violated their territory by taking shots at him and his people—inside his own establishment at that—and injuring three individuals in the process. Drip was ready to mobilize with his crew and take action. The question lingered: who ordered the hit? It was a question that demanded an answer. However, in the heat of the moment, Drip, Monk, Body, Animal, Hound Jr, Cold Heart, and the rest of the crew, were ready to shoot first and ask questions later.

After conducting one final walk through of the bar to ensure no victims remained and collecting the bullet casings for evidence, the police departed and headed to hospital. Their aim was to interview the individuals who had been shot, provided they were available for questioning.

Chapter 9

The police arrived at the hospital. They'd been provided with the name of each victim. Immediately, the cops were alerted by the department, that the man mentioned in the tip who'd been shot, had an outstanding warrant for his arrest. He faced two murder charges. Upon his emergence from surgery, and if he survived, he was to be arrested and taken to the county jail and booked.

The responding policeman contacted the Homicide Division, where the two detectives responsible for investigating the murder cases, reported to the hospital. They were Bill and Valco. Finally, they would have the opportunity to lay eyes on the young teenage suspect who'd eluded them for far too long. Although they had acquired a high school ID photo of Von, and had that identification confirmed by their confidential informant, Jeffery Toliver, also known as "JT," seeing him in person was different. They knew the shooting victim had to be the right person. Upon learning the names of the other two individuals who had been shot and approaching them in the examination rooms where they were being treated, the detective duo—Bill and Valco—immediately recognized Lily. He jarred his head in shock at the sight of her. The name didn't initially ring a bell, but seeing her brought back memories.

"Isn't this a surprise? I wasn't expecting to see you here," Bill said to Lily.

She glared angrily at him. Lily then spoke briefly.

"I don't have a damn thing to say to you," she said, then turned to face Valco. "You either."

"That's fine, Miss Dietrich. We feel the same way about you. But if you must know why we are here, the moment that son of yours—Trevon Dietrich Savage—gets his ass out of surgery and released from here, that little bastard will be arrested and taken to the county jail!"

"Fuck you!" Lily exclaimed loudly. "Y'all motherfuckas ain't got shit on my son! I promise you, we are both gonna walk on that charge! That shooting was a justifiable homicide. And the both you two dicks know it! So fall the fuck back!"

Bill looked on at her and smiled sinisterly.

"How about if I tell you that, we not only want your son for one murder. We want him for another as well. How do you explain that? Your ass can't cover for him on both, now can you!" Bill responded to her with a look of grimace etched across his face.

Lily could offer nothing to say behind Bill's revelation.

Hound Jr. then entered the examination room where Lily was being badgered. "Everything good with you, Lily?" he asked her.

"Not hardly, Cornelius! These two bumble-fucks, harassing me!"

Both Bill and Valco jarred their head at Hound Jr's presence.

"And who are you?" Valco asked. He and Bill took note of the physical similarities between Hound Jr. and the picture they had of Von.

"I'm Cornelius Savage Jr. She's the mother of my son, Trevon Savage. What's y'all issue with her?"

"You got some pair of balls, don't you buddy?" Valco stated. He then wrote down his name.

"We're just advising her, as we will you too, that when that son of you two comes out of surgery and able to leave the hospital, he won't be going home. His ass . . . will be going to jail!"

"They say Vonnie is wanted for two homicides, Cornelius," said Lily.

Hound Jr. had a very disturbing look out his face now. He felt the need to briefly address Bill's remark.

"Why are y'all bothering her? Is there a legal issue you need to take up with her or something?"

"If that was the case, we'd go through the DA's office. Besides, we've already made an arrest of her. Now, we're looking to have our day in court at some point next year," Bill stated.

"Okay. Then . . . leave her be. Save all you have for that day in court," Hound Jr. replied.

"You say you're Cornelius Savage Jr, correct?" Bill lastly asked.

"Cornelius Savage Jr. Indeed," he retorted.

Bill turned his head to have a look at Valco. He then nodded.

"I've written that down already, Bill," Valco clarified.

The two officers then exited the examination room and went towards the area where they were attending to Von. The authority was given by Bill to the officer in charge there: "DO NOT RELEASE! Arrest and detain for two counts of murder."

Bill also confiscated Von's personal effects upon his arrival at the hospital. They took his phone, wallet, car keys, and would have Von's car towed and impounded. Now, they had the authority to search everything Von possessed, including his phone records and any forms of identification found in his wallet and car. Von had more problems now than he could have imagined. Preparation for this day wasn't on his agenda prior to.

****

One Day Later . . .

Von miraculously survived the impact of those two hollow point bullets penetrating his body. He was indeed a fortunate young man. One bullet pierced his stomach cleanly, while the other came perilously close to his heart, lodging just an inch away. Surgery successfully repaired the internal damage and halted the internal bleeding. Von had lost a significant amount of blood and had flat lined four times before medical professionals stabilized his pulse and blood pressure. The quick thinking and decisive action of his family members who rushed him to receive medical attention in their car, undoubtedly saved his life. Waiting for an ambulance would have likely resulted in Von's death. He needed to remain in recovery until fully stable. However, thereafter, he would inevitably face incarceration in the county jail.

All of Von's visitors were turned away per police orders; no one, not even his mother, father, grandparents, or sisters, was allowed to see him anymore. When he regained consciousness, the police informed him that he was under arrest, which infuriated Von. Additionally, they informed him that they had possession of his phone, wallet, and car, and discovered his fake ID materials, along with a loaded gun and an assault rifle—an AR-15 Bushmaster—containing Black Rhino bullets. This discovery dealt a serious blow to his chances of obtaining freedom, as he now had more issues to contend with amidst the prevailing circumstances.

****

Drip had gathered his top associates at the penthouse; to include Hound Jr, Monk, Body, Animal, Pervis, Cold Heart, and Kenny, who was Drip's Aunt Mary's son. Mary is the sister of Drip and Monk's dad, Ishmael. They convened to discuss and devise a strategy to retaliate—but against whom exactly though?

Drip possessed footage from the surveillance cameras of *the Ozone*, which they watched repeatedly. None of them could identify the face of the brown-skinned shooter, and they had no clue about the intended target either. It could've been anyone present in the picture section at that time. However, judging from the video, the shooter's aim seemed directed at Drip, Monk, Hound Jr, or Von. Either one could have been on someone's hit list. They lacked clarity. The first shot missed, compelling the shooter to continue firing, resulting in the two females being hit. Perhaps those bullets were meant for them as well? Who knows!

Drip then began speaking more.

"Anybody got an idea who the shooter was? Y'all recognize the face?" he asked.

Everyone indicated NO with their heads

This also turned out to be a rare occasion for Drip and the crew. It was essential to have all of his most trusted people in one place at the same time, especially so to prevent from exposing Pervis to anyone present he had no knowledge of. They all needed to become acquainted.

Pervis had recently transitioned from being a uniformed lieutenant police officer to becoming a plain-clothed detective. He now served as part of the homicide unit, investigating cases of murder mostly. His jurisdiction was over south Philly.

Drip continued.

"Anybody got enemies you didn't know you had? Pissed anybody off lately? I'm only speaking to those of us who were shot at."

"Nah, bro. Not that we know of," Monk responded first.

"What about you, Cold?"

"Not to my knowledge, Drip. Whoever that nigga was that did the shooting, looked like he had a purpose. He meant business. And our response to that has gotta mean business too. Ain't no doubt about that. I'm ready to get busy, Drip!" Cold Heart stated.

"Oh, we about to do that for sure. We just need to identify our targets!" Drip said.

"You want my opinion, bro?" Animal chimed in to ask.

"Speak your peace, bro."

"You know me. I go in hard whenever there's work to be done. This situation ain't no different. All you gotta do is, say go. And we can go out and hit any and everybody who you *feel* like gave the order to come in your spot and shot your people. Just give us a list of names, and say *Go!*" Animal declared.

"I just got out the pen Monday, fam. And here it is, not even a week later, and I've got tough decisions to make. Something definitely gotta be done. Because my son and his mom was caught in the line of fire. And I ain't having none of that shit! So here we are, fam, in yet another situation, like the times before!" Hound Jr stated.

"But this time we ain't gotta get our hands dirty, fam. We got troops for that now. And, we got inside connections to help us track down who we may be looking for," responded Drip. He took a look over at Pervis as he stated the last sentence.

The eight of them continued to sit at the table, with Drip positioned at the head. Surrounding him were his family and his associates and friends of the family. While to his right sat designated family members. The seating order was specific. Von's seat remained conspicuously empty. Therefore, leaving the question to linger: when would Vonnie seize the opportunity to claim his rightful place at the table Drip had arranged? And to Drip's left, was specific seating for his associates.

Drip proved to be a mastermind in his ways and a calculated thinker. He had serious plans and clear visions. And everyone present that day either played a part in his schemes, or would soon be involved.

Drip cautioned everyone to remain vigilant and prepared. He hinted at compiling a list of individuals who would soon face consequences. Payback was inevitable.

****

Monk and Cold Heart departed from Drip's place and made their way to Williamsport to be with Tangee and Shayla. Their phone conversations with the girls had been brief, informing them of Von and others being shot. Cori, overwhelmed, teetered on the brink of losing her composure. Temporarily, she'd succumbed to a deep state of depression. A wave of relief washed over Cori upon learning that Von survived the ordeal, though he faced impending incarceration in the county jail, charged with murders.

Monk and Cold Heart, however, prioritized ensuring the smooth operation of their affairs. They understood the necessity for business to continue uninterrupted, and they bore the responsibility for its seamless execution.

Meanwhile, Ron would assume Von's position in upstate PA, already familiar with the town and the territory they controlled. He, along with his twin cousins—Khaddafi and Khalil—would spend a lot of their time there, away from the city, leaving Lonnie and Kareem with full control over the West Philly locations.

Lonnie and Kareem bolstered their ranks by enlisting family members and close friends onto the team. They had their areas on lock, and faced no opposition from rival factions or law enforcement. Fortunately, Lonnie had a female cousin who was a cop, allowing them to establish a connection with a certain male cop who acted as a double agent within both law enforcement and the underworld. Although Lonnie and Kareem had never met Drip, they recognized him as the enigmatic figure-head orchestrating events from the shadows. There was no question about who supplied them; Drip's reputation preceded him, although they had yet to meet him face-to-face. However, that meeting would happen soon. Despite facing setbacks such as one of their own being shot and arrested, the team remained resolute and determined to press forward with their operations.

Chapter 10

Three Years Later . . .

Von was finally released from the hospital and taken straight to the county jail. Upon being booked on the two murder charges against him, he found himself in the interrogation room, seated and handcuffed to the metal table there. Familiar with the formalities of such situations, Von mentally prepared himself for the interrogation process.

His anticipation was not in vain, as Bill Hilliard and Valente Canelo aka Valco—the two homicide detectives investigating the case—wasted no time delving directly into things. They entered the room promptly, eager to begin questioning Von.

"I'm detective Bill Hilliard. And he's my partner, Valente Canelo. To get straight to the point, kid, this is a very serious situation you've found yourself in—"

"I'm not a kid. Please don't call me that. A'ight!" Von cut in to say.

Bill's leering gaze bore down on him, exuding an unsettling intensity, interpreting Von's demeanor as laden with sarcasm and disrespect. Bill's countenance shifted, now inclined towards a more assertive and incisive approach in handling the two-murder suspect.

"*I'm* the one who's gonna do all the checking in this scenario here. You got that!" Bill said.

"Like I said, man, I'm not a kid. But go ahead with what you gotta say. I can't wait to hear this. Ain't this a bitch! I'm the one who got shot. And then, y'all turn around, and book me while I'm at the hospital, before I had a chance to be thoroughly healed. What type of shit is this?"

"The type of shit us great policemen do to people we want for charges of murder," Valco said in retort.

Bill proceeded to extract a gun and bullets from the paper bag he had brought along. The weapon and ammo was in a plastic bag and tagged as evidence. He methodically placed each item on the table, drawing out the suspense of the moment to an almost unbearable degree.

Von recognized the gun as his own, yet maintained a stoic silence, acquiescing to the detectives as they continued with their procedural formalities.

"It took some time for us to figure out who you were. But we finally did," stated Bill.

"Sir, I still haven't been told why am I here. Why was I arrested?"

Bill jarred his head at Von's words.

"You haven't?"

"No! I haven't. So why don't you two do your jobs, and make me aware of what you locked me up for, won't you? That'll be really nice of you. Now stop wasting my time and speak."

"I am compelled to inform you, as I'm sure you're aware, that your mother, Lillian Dietrich, was arrested and charged with complicity in the murder of her ex-boyfriend, Bernard Nichols. However, it is you who we have in custody as the perpetrator at this point, not her. Moreover, we possess confidential intelligence and substantial evidence implicating you as the assailant in the shooting death of Kavon Lassiter. Additionally, an assault rifle, this pistol and these bullets that's linked to the murder of a police officer and others, were discovered in your vehicle. Interestingly enough, we suspect that the black Dodge Magnum currently held in impound was the same vehicle involved in the altercation with Kavon Lassiter, wherein you allegedly shot him at close range in the head, killing him, all because he accidentally bumped into your car and took out a headlight. Now what do you say to that?" Bill conveyed with grave seriousness.

"That's three confidential informants we have, Bill. Not one," Valco chimed in to say.

"Thanks for the correction, Valco," Bill acknowledged, and continued. "Three people who witnessed you shoot Lassiter."

"That's not proof I did anything."

"That's sufficient evidence to detain you until we can further establish your involvement in all aspects of the case. Initially, we encountered difficulties in tracking you down, as we were unfamiliar with your identity and appearance, due to your youth and lack of a criminal record or driver's license. However, someone suggested checking school records, which led us to you. Interestingly, it appears that your father has come to the attention of federal authorities, who now have their own agenda to pursue in due course. But there you have it. That's the reason for your arrest. Furthermore, as we proceed with our investigation, we may find cause to add additional murder charges to the two already against you. These Black Rhino cop-killer bullets, which have been linked to numerous homicides across Philadelphia City, are a significant concern for the police commissioner and the Mayor. They have been relentless in pressuring us about these extremely lethal rounds. Regular bullets causing deaths are one matter. But the use of Black Rhino bullets elevates the seriousness of the situation. This is something we absolutely cannot tolerate."

"When do I see a judge about bail?"

"Bail! What bail? You may as well forget all about that!" Bill exclaimed vehemently.

"What about a lawyer?" Von further asked.

"If you do not have funds to retain a lawyer, one will be appointed to represent you. And judging from the information we've been provided about you and your Savage family, we'll expect for you to afford an attorney. All that narcotic y'all moving!" Bill stated.

"You're in deep shit, Trevon. Really deep shit!" Valco said.

"How can I be in deep shit and I ain't do what y'all accusing me of?"

"You don't have to confess to anything. We have more than enough evidence, I'm sure, to get a guilty verdict on everything. If you don't plea out before a trial is had!" Bill boasted.

"Humph!" Von huffed. "I'm an innocent man. I won't be taking a plea on nothing! I want to talk with a lawyer. I'm done here."

"Not a problem, buddy. We're done here too. I'll be seeing you and your momma in court, son," Bill remarked as he began to put the gun and bullets back into the paper bag.

"If you don't end up dropping all the charge before we get to that point," Von said.

"That won't be happening at all, kid!" Bill fired back and gave Von a smirk before walking out the room.

They had additional information about Von and his associates. The two detectives were determined to secure arrest warrants. Additionally, they sought to acquire crucial evidence from the various locations and other phone records linked to Von's phone. His arrest proved to be advantageous for them. Bill and Valco harbored devious intentions to maximize their advantage to the fullest extent possible.

****

One Week Later . . .

The two pregnant cousins, Chloe and Rosa Dominquez, finally moved in together and made it a duty to manage everything until the outcome of Von's situation was known. Both were at the eight-month mark of their pregnancies and would soon be giving birth. Despite their condition, they continued to work and would soon be placed on maternity leave. The question weighing on their minds was what to do now while Von was incarcerated on two murder charges and firearms possession. Life had to go on, for better or for worse. Chloe reached out to Lily and invited her over. She and Rosa needed to have a serious discussion, and Lily obliged.

Once seated in the apartment, the conversation commenced. It was the second time Lily had the opportunity to meet Rosa, although she was already acquainted with Chloe.

"Hey, Lily. I'm glad you came by to talk with us," Chloe said warmly as she embraced Lily.

Rosa followed suit with a hug of her own.

"I'm glad to be here, Chloe. And I finally have the chance to meet you again, Rosa. Correct?" Lily responded.

"That's correct," Rosa affirmed.

Lily looked on at the two simultaneously, pleasantly serving them with a smile. She shook her head, seemingly astonished by the situation her son had created.

"What is it, Lily?" Chloe inquired, smiling. She understood Lily's thought process and had an inclining sense of what she might be thinking.

"My-my-my! What in the world has that son of mine got going now?" Lily exclaimed, chuckling softly. She took a moment to absorb it all.

Chloe and Rosa exchanged smiles in response.

"Vonnie's got it going on, Miss Lily. Like, for real, he does. And we love every bit of what we have put together," Rosa stated.

"It must be nice. But look, let's talk about what we need to do moving forward, shall we?" Lily declared.

"Let's do that," Chloe uttered.

She and Rosa sat together on the love seat while Lily occupied the single chair across from them. Lily, observing their show of solidarity, knew then and there that the two were in total agreement with their shared poly lifestyle.

"Okay, so, I have a good idea what this is all about. You two want to know the situation with my son? And where the support for those babies gonna come from? Simply put . . . Vonnie's got a tough war to fight. He won't be getting a bail. They're gonna keep him there in jail until all this is said and done. He should have a good outcome though. But we'll know more on what's the pass. Right now, they got him booked on two counts of murder. But that's not gonna stick, and I've gotta do all I can to see to it that these three babies my boy got on the way are taken care of until they arrive," Lily stated.

"Three babies!" both Chloe and Rosa asked at the same time.

Lily tilted her head at their reaction.

"It's my turn too, Miss Lily," Chloe said.

Lily looked at them, pondering on the best course of action at the present moment. She didn't want Vonnie to be troubled and stressed any more than he already was, especially not about anything related to two females he's dealing with, and whom he eventually must confront to address the reality of the other baby they knew nothing about. So, Lily took it upon herself to handle the situation for him. That way, he wouldn't have to. Besides, Von had already confided everything to his mother. That occurred on the same night his dad returned home, and they all convened at his granddad Hound Sr.'s house.

Lily broached the topic subject. "Well, obviously, Vonnie's not here to update you two on everything he's dealing with. Fortunately, he has a mother who's willing to do that for him."

Chloe and Rosa exchanged a glance. Their silent way of communicating was a reminder to each other to maintain control and avoid getting upset.

"We wanna hear what you've got to tell us, Miss Lily," Chloe said.

"And we're mature enough to not get pissed at whatever you're gonna share with us. Vonnie don't need problems out of us," Rosa chimed in. "Not in the least."

"He definitely don't. Anyway, Vonnie was feeling himself a little too much at the beginning of the year. That's a natural thing for young men his age. He was involved with a lot of females. He said there's another young girl named Cori, who's pregnant too, just a month behind you both. From what I know, I've never seen her, only heard about her once. Apparently, she was hustling with him and they were making money together. Basically, he had her doing the things he didn't want either of you participating in. She's the one who had his car. The girl has her own place to live, too. As y'all know, he needed a stable body. The boy was all over the place how he saw fit. But that's the gist of that. What else do you two feel like you need to know? Speak now or forever hold your peace. Because we're not going back over this again. Ever!" Lily stated.

Chloe and Rosa exchanged glances, still processing all that Lily had said. They both shook their heads in disbelief. But the fact remained regarding Vonnie. At the time he was frolicking with multiple women, he had no relationship obligations to any of them. He exercised his sexual freedom as he pleased, with no restrictions. The young man had exotic genes and held the potential to create physical enigmas. How lucky they were!

Rosa offered to speak up first, echoing Lily's sentiments. "We're not tripping behind that, Miss Lily. We know first-hand how good the sex is with your son, and what a good person he is. We just don't want to navigate this situation alone. If Vonnie not gonna be around, we need to know his family will be. That's all."

Chloe nodded in agreement with what Rosa said.

"I wouldn't be here, Rosa, if I didn't intend to be around for you two. The three of you for that matter. And whether y'all know it or not, Vonnie's father was released from prison about four weeks ago. He's back, you know. We still have a solid bond with each other. His family is fairly well-off. Plus, you two have family and jobs. So, everything's gonna be good. I just need you two to be strong and not abandon my baby."

"We're not, Miss Lily. Vonnie has our undeniable support. Our first babies are gonna be by him. He's gonna forever be a part of our lives," Chloe stated emphatically.

"I'm glad to know y'all think like this and that we're all on the same page. But hey, I've gotta go. I've got a meeting with a lawyer at two. Y'all got money, right?" Lily inquired.

"Vonnie gave us twenty-five thousand each. And before that, he had us holding money for him too," Chloe informed Lily.

"How much?" Lily asked.

"I've been holding thirty thousand," Rosa revealed.

"And you?"

"I had thirty-five on top of the twenty-five he gave me," said Chloe.

Damn! Vonnie had that kind of money lying around, Lily thought.

"So the both of you together holding onto over a hundred thousand dollars together for my son?"

"Yeah. I guess!" Chloe responded.

"Y'all please put the money away in a bank or some other safe place. Okay? Please do. And call me when y'all need more or simply wanna talk. Now, y'all come on. Give me a hug. And let me get on my way to see me and my baby's lawyer," Lily stated.

Lily hugged Chloe and Rosa. She kissed them both on the forehead and proceeded on her way to see Levi Jacobson.

Chloe and Rosa felt a greater sense of confidence and assurance after their conversation with Lily. Throughout the whole talk, they didn't touch on the shooting. All they cared about was that Vonnie was alive and okay, that he would survive to meet his babies when they were born, and that everything would be okay. Lily's wounds were healing well.

Chapter 11

Von managed to contact his homie, Cold Heart. Drip gave Von's lawyer a list of phone numbers. Each of them had an initial beside it, a code only Von would understand, indicating the specific contact.

Levi Jacobson charged a retainer fee of $600K to represent Von. Hound Sr. and Jr. pooled their resources to cover the cost. Levi immediately began investigating the crimes Von was accused of committing. However, he couldn't access all the details the prosecutor had until the discovery package was issued. Patience was imperative.

Once Von contacted Cold Heart, they talked about all the people Cold Heart needed to get in touch with, especially those who owed money. One notable name was Jeffrey Toliver, aka JT. They hadn't seen or heard from him for quite some time now, yet he owed Von for two bricks of heroin he'd been fronted, totaling more than $50K. Von demanded payment, or consequences would follow.

"When was the last time you saw or heard from the nigga JT?" Von asked.

"JT? It's been a while. Maybe the day we were all at your spot," Cold Heart responded.

"Damn! That long?"

"Yeah. It's been a minute. I thought maybe he moved out of town or something."

"Nah. That nigga owe me a grip. For two units, to be exact."

"That is a grip, ain't it? What you need me to do?"

"Find that nigga and get that paper he should have for me. It's been long enough."

"I'm on it, bro. I know where his people live. His mom."

"Check. And if you have to, slide through the spot we were looking to set him up at."

"Where?"

"The spot on Eighth and girl's best friend. There's a bar there. He and a few of his young cousins used to get money that way," Von explained.

"No doubt, bro. I'mma make it my business to handle that business for you. A'ight."

"Word."

"But other than that, how you been feeling? We still ain't got no clue who did the shooting. But when we do . . . That's all I'mma say."

"Yeah, I'm good, bro. Everything been going good on your end? How are the girls in the port?"

"For the most part, everything flowing smoothly. Me and Monk been managing well. And your girl—Cori—is about to drop soon. Has she been able to come see you yet?"

"Nah. Not yet. She's been writing to me like crazy though. Everything still good with you and Shay?"

"Yeah, we are. She wants too much of my time though. Her situation kinda prevents that."

"I forgot about that."

"Yeah. She's got that still going on. I balance my time between her and Tiona, between Philly and the Port."

"Oh. You and Tiona. I'm glad to hear what y'all got is still holding up. That's a good thing, bro."

"No doubt, bro. And I'm sure you and Monyetta still locked in, right?"

"No doubt. She's been by my side. Her and Kiki got a solid bond. So 'Yetta won't be going nowhere, bro. We in it to win it," Von stated.

"You have one minute left!" the phone system alerted them.

"Yo, bro, this phone 'bout to cut us off. I'mma get back at you again soon. Stay up out there and much love!" Von stated.

"No doubt, my nigga. You do the same. Much love. One!" said Cold Heart

"One!"

The call concluded.

Cold Heart then made up his mind to go out and track down the guy JT, and collect the cash he owed Von. It was necessary that he do.

****

The two police detectives—Bill and Valco—acquired crucial information that they could leverage against potential suspects. Upon unlocking Von's phone, they identified a repeated number from the records of previously arrested individuals (J-Dubb and Cori). A state-wide search on the phone number revealed its connection to an apartment in Williamsport. The lease listed the names Cori Allen and Tayshawn Jefferson as occupants—a male and female couple. The name "Tayshawn Jefferson" matched one of the ID cards found in Von's car, leading Bill and Valco to conclude it was a fake. They obtained a warrant to raid the apartment, and action was taken.

With a "No-Knock" forced entry, the officers breached the door. State Troopers and Williamsport Police combed through the apartment, but found no one present. They meticulously searched the premises and discovered half a kilo of heroin, three handguns and $20K in cash. Somebody had to be charged, and Cori, listed on the lease, was likely to bear the blame. Von couldn't be charged, as "Tayshawn Jefferson," was obviously a false identity.

In addition, the cops discovered genuine ID cards belonging to the girls. One belonged to the "Shayla Allen Suspect" they were already looking for. Bill and Valco were certain that they were onto something significant. All that remained was to conduct ballistics checks on the guns to determine if they were linked to any crimes, and to locate their targets.

Meanwhile, Cori went into premature labor with Von's child. The baby's early arrival granted them a temporary stroke of luck. Their elderly white female neighbor informed the authorities that the previous evening, the resident of the apartment had gone to the hospital for childbirth, potentially aiding them in locating her, which indeed, they did.

Shayla and Tangee had already departed for Philadelphia the day before to fetch Cori and Shayla's mother, intending to bring them, along with Cori's two existing children, to Williamsport. Tamika—Cori's friend—remained by her side when the police unexpectedly entered the room to arrest her. Aunt Shirley was also present. Shirley and Tamika, promptly contacted Shayla, to relay the situation and advise her to keep away. Cori was now en route back to jail, facing charges of heroin and firearms possession, sinking deeper into trouble once again, and booked on the heroin and firearms offenses. She was now in a really troubling predicament.

Cori named her baby girl Trevonya Cori Savage. Before her arrest, she had the opportunity to relinquish her parental rights over baby Trevonya to her mother, placing her fate in the hands of the legal system. This turned out to be a wise decision, to prevent the state from taking custody of the kids.

****

The ballistic test results revealed that one of the pistols recovered had been used in the shooting incident where a man and a young girl were the victims. Tragically, the girl lost her life, while the man survived. The victims were identified as Feezy Richardson and his daughter, Dedra. Shayla's fingerprints were discovered all over the gun. Previously, she'd been arrested for involvement in a street fight, though she was misidentified as another individual in the police database. Her warrant status transitioned from being wanted for questioning, to being considered the actual shooter. With little recourse, she had no choice but to inform Cold Heart of the dire situation. Tangee and Monk were also informed of the escalating circumstances. Everything seemed to be unravelling swiftly for them. It was a downward spiral to the bottom of a pit.

Chapter 12

October 2009 . . .

Shayla and Tangee returned to the motel in Camden once more, finding a certain level of comfort in that familiar place. Shayla felt the urgency to speak with Cold Heart in person and wasted no time in contacting him. He promptly made his way to meet her.

As they convened inside, Tangee remained present to witness the unfolding conversation. "Cold! We've got even more problems than we anticipated, bro!" Shayla exclaimed as soon as they began to talk.

"What do we have now that you didn't mention when they booked Cori?" he inquired.

Shayla met his gaze unwavering as they delved into the pressing matters at hand. Meanwhile, Tangee sat on the bed, observing the exchange. Tears welled up in Shayla's eyes as the weight of their predicament became evident, and she began to weep.

"What the fuck is it, Shay? Talk! And don't hold back! Tangee know what we all got goin' on!"

"The gun, Cold. They found it!" Shayla revealed.

"They found all three of y'all guns. Which one are you talking about?" Cold Heart now demanded.

Shayla hesitated. She wasn't sure if she could muster enough courage to reveal everything to Cold Heart.

"Talk, Shay!"

"My gun, Cold," Shayla replied.

He shrugged, his face contorted in confusion. "What's so different about *that* gun compared to the other two?" he asked.

"Because, Cold, that's the gun I used when I went to deal with ol' boy," Shayla confessed.

Cold Heart took a moment to process the gravity of the situation she was talking about. Suddenly, realization dawned on him.

"Say what, Shay! Tell me you're bullshitting!"

Tangee couldn't help but shake her head at her friend's words.

Shayla remained silent, refusing to utter a word.

"Shay, why the fuck you didn't you get rid of that gun? What the fuck was you thinking! Are you stupid or something!" Cold Heart's frustration boiled over as he verbally chastised her.

"Answer me, Shay! Why the fuck you didn't toss that shit, or give it to me to handle?" he demanded.

"I don't know, Cold. I should have. But I didn't. And I'm so sorry. Please forgive me."

"Shay! You know how serious this shit is right now!" Cold Heart's tone remained stern.

As Shayla continued to cry, Cold Heart continued to lay into her.

"A little girl died, Shay! And the cops don't take that shit too lightly about those kids being killed in the line of fire. And on top of Vonnie being shot and booked, your sister—his girl—has landed herself back in trouble, just after having the man's baby. And now this shit with you. What the fuck!"

"What am I supposed to do now?" Shayla asked, her voice filled with desperation.

Cold Heart slowly shook his head, unsure of how to respond.

"I don't know. I can't say right now. You can't go back to Williamsport. You can't come out too much in Philly. You gotta do something to make money. We're gonna figure something out though. We ain't got no other options. Tangee is the only one of all of us all, who hasn't really had any trouble with the cops. I'm sure Monk gonna do all he can to keep her that way. And as your dude, I've gotta do what I can to help you out of this situation. Plus, I've got Vonnie to help out too."

"I'm with her, Cold. Shay's my girl. I've gotta have her back on point, no matter what," Tangee interjected.

"That's a good thing. However, Shay, the most viable option for you to earn money seems to be setting up here and generating income through your phone," Tangee suggested. "Alternatively, we could go back up to Williamsport, and I could secure an apartment in my name."

"That'll work too. Y'all gonna be here and there together anyway, so what the fuck! But how the fuck the cops know who y'all were? Why did they hit y'all anyway?" Cold Heart asked.

Shayla and Tangee were at a loss for words regarding the specific target. They themselves were unsure.

"We can't say, Cold. We really don't know," Shayla responded

"Look, I'mma keep in touch. Y'all be cool, hit me up if you need something, and y'all change out those phones and get new numbers. A'ight!" he lastly stated, giving Shayla a hug, a quick peck on the lips, and a pat on the ass.

He then left, heading to meet with Drip and Monk to discuss the Williamsport situation.

****

While gathered at Drip's penthouse, Monk, Hound Jr, Cold Heart, and Body convened to discuss the recent events that happened at the bar. Following the shooting at *the Ozone*, city's policy mandated a sixty-day closure of Drip's bar, as authorities investigated the incident. The uncertainty surrounding the shooter's identity infuriated Drip, leading him to adopt a cautious demeanor, which he found unsettling. Drip would be particularly disconcerted by what Cold Heart was about to disclose. Seated around the small table bar in the living room corner, Monk provided the latest updates on the situation. "Bro. We've got problems up in the 'Port."

"Oh, we do? How so?" Drip inquired.

"The cops hit the girls. They found work, money, and guns."

"Anybody got booked?"

"Yeah. The chick Vonnie was dealing with."

Hound Jr. knew nothing about this particular female or operation in upstate. He jerked his head at the mention of his son's name.

Drip and Monk continued.

"On what?" Drip asked.

"A half unit and the hammers. The worst part about that for her is, she just had their baby," Monk informed him.

Hound Jr. jumped to the occasion to speak out now, being informed of his first grandchild being born. "Oh yeah! So one of my three grand babies is here already. That's what up there. I've gotta get in touch with her people so I can see the baby. A boy or a girl?' Hound Jr. asked.

"A little girl, fam," Monk replied. "Congratulations."

"No doubt."

"But look, Von. Cold got something he need to let you know. Go ahead and let him in on this," Monk urged Cold Heart

Cold Heart spoke up. "I'll cut through the chase, Drip. One of the guns the cops found belonged to the chick I deal with. It's got a body on it!" Cold Heart said bluntly.

Drip tilted his head, signaling Cold Heart to continue.

"She's the same one from before, if you remember? The one who got cut, and got at her boyfriend behind it."

"Talking about the one who . . . " Drip paused, mimicking the height of the little girl he referred to. "The five-year-old and the boyfriend daddy?" Drip clarified.

"Yeah, man. That one. And more than likely, they gonna link the banger to her."

"Your girl?" Drip asked.

"Yep . . . My girl," Cold Heart affirmed.

"And, she's the one who did the thing with you, Body and Animal too, right?"

Cold Heart nodded in confirmation.

"Ah, man. This ain't good, Cold. It's definitely not. We've gotta act quickly. Who knows what she'd say once they get to her. And we can't have this. It's all on you, Cold. You already know she knows too much. You and her don't have any kids, do you?"

"Nah. We ain't got no babies together, bro. She don't have no kids at all."

"Well . . . as bad as it may sound, she's gotta be taken care of, bro. Like immediately!" Drip stated.

"No doubt, bro. I'll take care of it in a few days. Monk gonna be sure to let you know when it's done," Cold Heart assured.

"And be sure to fix it to where they find her. That way, all she knew and any evidence against her, would go away when they finally do identify her, a'ight!" Drip ordered.

"For sure, bro. It's done," Cold Heart concluded on the matter, then fell silent as the meeting continued. The circumstances of the situation warranted the decision that Drip made. He was right about dealing with it in this way.

Chapter 13

Chloe was alone in the apartment she shared with Rosa. Rosa herself had gone to spend part of her day with her parents. They often got parenting tips from their mothers and female relatives, and she was looking to gain the wisdom that they had to offer.

Seated and watching TV, Chloe decided to answer a call from someone she felt conflicted about at this point. It was Raul. They engaged in conversation for a while, with Raul expressing his desire to check on her and her well-being.

"Hey. Chloe! How have you been?" Raul asked.

"I've been good, Raul," Chloe replied, somewhat reluctantly.

"That's good to know. When are you due?" Raul pressed.

"Soon," Chloe responded.

"Soon, huh? And how long you plan on holding back on me? I'm not gonna stop believing you're not carrying my baby until I know for sure," Raul insisted.

"I'm not pregnant by you, Raul. This is Vonnie's baby. And why do you insist on thinking the way you do?"

"Because, I still love you, Chloe. And I'm deeply concerned about you. That dude you dealing with is facing not one, but *two* murder charges. Not to mention the guns. And I feel the need to be there for you. If you want my opinion, your so-called boyfriend, ain't never coming home," Raul stated emphatically. His aim was to instill a sense of dread about Von's grim reality, hoping to ease closer and, in his view, save the day.

"Raul, why have you already 'convicted' Vonnie before he had the chance to go to court? And if you called to talk to me or check on me, as you claim, then you have no business discussing Vonnie."

"I'm just stating the obvious about him. That's all. Beating one murder is hard enough as it is. But two! Now that . . . That's a tall task there. But I'll keep it about you and me for the most part."

"Thank you. That'll be better. And if you wanna mention his name again, you can start by maybe telling me who shot Vonnie, his mom, and the other girl?" Chloe asked.

"If you asking if I was the one who did it, nah, it wasn't me. I can't tell you nothing about that. Whoever it was, meant business. And I don't know too much about those people. But the guy who owned the bar, he's not to be taken lightly. From what the streets saying," Raul explained.

"I don't have any idea who those people are either. His dad got out not long before the day he got shot. I haven't even met him yet. But anyway, was there something in particular you needed to talk about, or did you just want to talk? Because I've got too much other stuff to focus on. My bills need to be paid soon. My mind's been on that. If you're concerned about me and my well-being, that's a good place to start," Chloe stated.

"Chloe, you mean to tell me, all that money dude made when he was out here, he didn't leave you no money to take care what you need to?" Raul questioned.

"I didn't say that. And again, let's keep the conversation about you and me. Or I'm gonna have to end this call," Chloe warned.

Chloe was quietly hoping to get some financial support from Raul. She believed it would be enough to tide her over a few months after she had the baby. Opposite the money she already had. Despite her reluctance to admit it, she still had a special kind of affection for Raul. After all, he was her first—the one who took her virginity. Such experiences often left an indelible mark on one's heart.

"Look, what do you need? A few dollars to pay bills with?" Raul asked.

"That'll be nice."

"And what I get in return?" Raul pressed.

"What do you mean, *what do you get in return?* The *fuck!*" Chloe retorted. "I'm pregnant, Raul. And not about to be with you sexually."

"I'll take a blow job. Or you can just get naked for me, and let me beat my dick until I blow a load on that big ass of yours. And how are you pregnant, but haven't had any sexual desires? I thought that's when females want it most," Raul said to her.

He worked his request in a way he knew would make her laugh. Raul always had the ability with her, and knew that if he were to get her to himself, he'd be able to have her give in as usually. Pregnant pussy was some of the best. There had never been an opportunity for him to experience his share of any. Maybe the moment was at hand.

"You stupid, Raul!" she giggled. "You want me to get naked, so you can beat your dick, and blow a load on my ass cheeks. If I get naked over you, your ass gonna have to bury your face between my legs and eat the shit out of this wet ass pussy of mine. And I'm hoping that some dope female rapper eventually make a song in the future 'bout that."

"Huh!"

"Wet ass pussy, Raul."

"That would be a nice name for a song, wouldn't it?" Raul said.

"It sure would. But look, where you want me to meet you?"

"I got my own place now. Not too far from your mom's house."

"Well, just meet me at my mom's house. I gotta stop by there anyway. I'll text you when I get there."

"A'ight. I'll be there."

"And you better have some money for me too. I could use it, Raul!" Chloe remarked.

"I'mma have some for you."

"Okay. I'll see you in a few."

"A'ight," Raul said.

The call between the two came to an end. They then prepared to meet up.

****

Hound Jr. made significant progress in the free world since his return home. The money he entrusted to his kid's mother had proven tremendously helpful. He'd visited the same Range Rover dealership where Drip had purchased his vehicle, and leased one himself—a royal blue, fully loaded 4.6 edition.

Additionally, Hound Jr. had secured a lease for a place to stay. Although he could've continued living with his father in the large spacious home he owned, the son valued his privacy. Moreover, he wanted to ensure that Daniella would be in a comfortable position when they eventually moved in together.

The location he chose to live was already familiar to him—it was an apartment complex within a gated community located up in Bucks County, Middletown Township, Pennsylvania; about thirty minutes outside Philly. Known as Racquet Club Town Houses, it exuded a posh and affluent environment that he felt good about living in, as well as being safe.

Hound Jr. was now prepared to carve his own path, making money and building his own empire of fame. No longer content to ride the coat tails of his cousin, Drip. While Drip had ascended to power with the foundation laid by

Hound Jr.'s efforts, and despite the fact that Drip owed him a debt that money couldn't repay, Hound Jr. harbored a burning desire to chart his own course once again, building his way up according to his own vision and methods.

Von contacted his dad from the county jail, employing their established method of communication to ensure their conversation remained undisclosed. He needed his father to collaborate with his trusted associate, Cold Heart, and others in their circle, to rectify the situation he had created and clean up the mess up. Von also sought their assistance in identifying the individuals responsible for his shooting and ensuring their disappearance—the perpetrators of the failed hit.

The dialogue between father and son was the beginning of many discussions to follow, as Von awaited trial.

"What's up, Pop? How you been, my G?" Von greeted to initiate.

"I'm good, son. Making moves in the right directions. Got a new ride now. A place in Bucks County too. How you holding up? Feeling better? Getting your strength back?"

"Oh yeah. I still haven't healed well enough to be let into general population. They got me in the infirmary. Shouldn't be too much longer though. Mom doing better, right? Whoever those clowns were, they made a *huge* mistake."

"Yeah, Mom's good. She wasn't hurt too bad. And I'm with you. That clown has to pay, whoever he is. But your mom is fine. We talk at least three times a week. We'll always be cool."

"What about grandpa and the family?" Von asked.

"Everybody's good, son. We're just waiting to see what your next moves gonna be. What do I need to do, or who do I need to get in touch with for you?" Hound Jr. asked.

"Get with my homie, Cold Heart, for me. He's out there handling business for me. And if anything, I would recommend you and him get together to make things happen, if you plan to take my place with Drip."

"No doubt, I plan to stick with my family. But the material he's got . . . It's not my style no more. It's a new thing taking its place in the world. Something you can take with you anywhere you go. Everybody likes it. And it's cheaper," Hound Jr. stated.

"I heard something about that. The vanilla flavored *ice-cream* you talking about, right?"

"Yeah, that's the one. I heard a lot about it when I was away. I saw a lot of it too. Nowhere near the material Drip got circulating, like the new wave of material. But look, we'll talk about all this at another time. What did they say about your charges?"

"I don't really know yet. I'm waiting on the discover now. There were two dick-head detectives who harassed me. They said something about having a confidential informant on one of the charges. I'll find out soon enough who that is. And if it's who I'm thinking, he won't be too hard to find. Now that I think back, I ain't seen a certain dude in a minute now. Nigga owe me money too," Von explained to his father.

"I'm familiar with those detectives you talking about. But, you need me and your homie, Cold, to get together?"

"Yeah, he's got a few stops to make for me and pick up some paper. Bro should be able to put you up on everything we got going on in our circle. You and Cold need to link up, I suggest. That way, once I make it outta here, y'all two should have things up and running smoothly. Especially for you, I mean from a position you don't have to be too involved. I'm sure you gonna have some type of legit business going by then."

"I definitely should. But look, hit me up later in the week, a'ight. I've gotta get my ass up and outta here. Its two in the afternoon already."

"A'ight, Pop. You be easy. And I love you, my G."

"Love you too, son. Be easy."

The call between father and son concluded on a positive note. Hound Jr. assured his son that he would fulfill whatever was needed without fail.

PART TWO

Chapter 14

Cold Heart contacted Shayla and told her to be ready by the time he arrived to pick her up. They had a trip to make, one to a location in upstate Pennsylvania. However, it wasn't Williamsport. It was to Scranton, Pennsylvania—a place where she would lay low and get back to making money, so to address the legal situation when the time came. Cold Heart informed her that he had family there and wanted to do business in this location. In the way he saw fit with the product they sold, just the two of them—he and her. Shayla was eager to prove her worth and show her loyalty to Cold Heart for staying by her side in such a troubling situation.

Cold Heart pulled up to the motel to pick up Shayla, but he wasn't in his own car. Instead, he arrived in a late 90's Chevy Monte Carlo. He called to let her know he was outside the room.

"Hello!" Shayla answered the phone.

"Hey. I'm out front," Cold Heart responded.

She glanced out the window, expecting to see Cold Heart's Firebird. It wasn't there.

"I don't see your car," she said.

"I'm in my other car. The blue one here," he said, then flicked the lights.

"Okay, come in and help me with my bags so I don't take so long."

"Just bring what you can, as much as you can. I gotta make an important call when I hang up with you."

"Alright." Shayla ended the call and hastened her pace to get inside the car and listen in on the important phone call her partner needed to make. She then exited the room with the majority of her belongings, knowing she would need two trips to the car and the room to retrieve all her property.

"Hey, sweetie," Shayla greeted as she settled into the car, leaning over to give him a kiss.

"What's good, boo?" Cold Heart replied, putting the car in gear to back out, and then pulling off.

He drove in the direction of Philly.

"I gotta make a quick stop somewhere. We're gonna hit the road after that, okay," he said.

"I was wondering why we didn't just head on up. But okay," Shayla responded.

They continued on towards the city.

"I see everything going well between Tangee and Monk," Shayla said, trying to make conversation along the ride.

The radio was on Power 99 and played the power mix at the nine o'clock hour. Shayla danced and grooved her upper body, arms, and head to the music. She felt the need to do something to dispel the nervousness she felt. She was ready to get out of the way and not allow the cops to have an opportunity to get a hand on her.

"Oh yeah. Those two there really got it going on," Cold Heart responded.

"Hell yeah, they do. They're down in Miami now on a vacation. She said Monk and Von got family down there. I wish I could go somewhere nice like that at some point in my life."

"Just be cool. We're gonna get a chance to do all of that and more. We just gotta continue to work hard and do all we gotta do to get to that level. Keep the faith. We're gonna get there."

"And I'm here with you to help you get us there. On God, I am!" Shayla turned to look at him, her gaze intense. A solemn expression etched her face as she pursed her lips and furrowed her eyebrows, revealing the depth of her determination. A solitary tear trickled down her left cheek, tracing a path over the ugly scar she bore. Cold Heart took a glance at her. The emotions resonated with him, but he refocused on the road ahead.

They arrived at their destination across the bridge—a row house in North Philly. Cold Heart parked in the dimly lit alley behind the building, the darkness more pervasive than usual.

"Hold up for a moment. I'll be back in a minute," he said to her.

"Please do. It's too dark here, and this neighborhood is dangerous. I ain't got nothing to protect myself with. So, please hurry back to me, Cold," Shayla pleaded, concern evident on her face.

Cold Heart merely smirked, exited the car, and strolled away, taking the keys with him. The night held a slight chill, befitting the late October weather.

An unsettling feeling washed over Shayla, reminiscent of the year before when she was wounded on Halloween day.

Five minutes stretched into ten, yet Cold had not returned. To compound Shayla's unease, the house Cold Heart walked into remained shrouded in darkness, giving off an abandoned aura, reminiscent of some trap house where junkies shot heroin or something. It appeared to be a haunted house of some sort to her.

She dialed Cold Heart's phone number, only to be met with a voice-mail. Trying again yielded the same result. Frustration mounting, she resorted to texting.

"I don't know what kind of games Cold thinks he's playing on me, but tonight ain't the time," she muttered to herself as she composed a lengthy message to Cold Heart.

Unbeknownst to her, a hooded figure stealthily approached from behind the car, slipping into her blind spot.

Bang!

A gunshot shattered the silence, piercing through the passenger side window. Shayla recoiled as the bullet struck the back of the head. Moments prior, her attention was momentarily diverted to the outgoing message. She never saw it coming. Her body lurched forward, colliding with the dashboard.

The assailant pried open the door, seizing Shayla's phone. *Bang . . . Bang!*

Two more shots echoed, targeting her head once more. With the deed done, the assailant fled, leaving the door ajar. It was apparent: the intent was for Shayla to be discovered. The problems she had created, the impending confrontations with the police, and everything else, all vanished with her demise. The cases against her would remain unsolved, with the perpetrator now silenced forever.

****

The Next Morning . . .

The Philadelphia Homicide Division received an urgent call from the Sanitation Department regarding a dead body discovered inside a car along their trash route in an alley. The grim discovery unfolded near the intersection of Germantown and Glenwood Avenues, falling under the investigative purview of Detectives Bill and Valco. Upon arrival at the scene, they found the crime unit already present. Officer Gavin Lowe provided a concise briefing to the detectives.

"This appears to be a targeted shooting," Lowe stated.

Bill and Valco, alongside Lowe, positioned themselves about five feet away from the car's passenger side, their gazes fixed on the lifeless form of the perceived female victim as they deliberated on the unfolding situation.

"How so?" Bill inquired in response to Lowe's statement.

"Well, for starters, the victim has three entry wounds to the back of the head."

"Wow! That is deliberate. Can you determine if the victim is male, female, or of unknown gender?" Bill questioned further.

"It's uncertain at this time. It appears to be a female, but we'll confirm once we get the body down to the coroner's office."

"Understood," Bill acknowledged.

The trio then approached the body. Bill donned a pair of latex gloves and carefully examined the bullet holes in the victim's head. A thick patch of dried blood marked the location of the wounds. He also noticed the victim's purse on the floor of the car, while the steering column seemed tampered with, possibly hot-wired or forcibly accessed with a screwdriver. Bill looked up at Lowe.

"We ran the plates already. The car was reported stolen two days ago," Lowe informed them.

"I had a hunch," Bill remarked, nodding.

"Anybody see or hear anything?" Valco asked.

"Nope. Not a soul. This neighborhood is notorious for drugs and crime. People here are more concerned about their next fix than anything else," Lowe explained, acknowledging the reality of the area's challenges, as a white male police veteran to a black male police veteran.

Both detectives were keenly aware of the pervasive poverty and decay that characterized the area. The moniker attributed to the location encapsulated its essence: the *Badlands*. Every aspect of the neighborhood epitomized its grim reputation. "That sounds like a systemic issue, Officer Lowe," Bill remarked to his colleague. "Every ethnic community seems to have its 'Bad Lands,' not just here in North Philadelphia."

As Bill spoke, the crime scene official diligently began the task of clearing the body from the car, preparing it to be collected and stored in the preloaded body bag.

Valco shook his head with a heavy heart (he has a sister himself) as he studied the female victim's face. There was a flicker of recognition, as if he might have known who she was.

"Hold up for a moment," Valco interjected, halting the crew in their motion to seal the body bag. He swiftly strode to the car he and Bill had used, retrieving a thick leather profile binder before returning to the group. Inside, he carried rogue photographs of the individuals sought on homicide charges, his memory serving as a reliable guide. Locating Shayla's picture, he pointed out a small mole on the right side of her forehead that served as a distinguishing feature.

"It's her, Bill. One of the girls we've been hunting for. The Richardson guy and daughter shooting victims," Valco informed his partner, directing his finger to the photo as he spoke.

"She has the same mole. Skin complexion matches also. We just need a positive ID," Bill commented.

"Definitely so. Minus the scar," Valco agreed, as another officer handed Bill an ID card.

"This might help," said the officer who offered.

"Yes, this is our girl, Shayla Allen. Now, we need to uncover exactly why was she executed. And that's putting it mildly. Three bullets to the head at close range is a clear execution," Bill remarked.

"What a tragedy!" Lowe interjected solemnly, proceeding to seal the body bag and load the victim's corpse into the van.

Bill and Valco documented the crime scene, taking notes and photographs before they were to return to their office to await the official report on the deceased female.

News reporters were now on the scene, necessitating the police to provide an account of the situation. Following this, the police would have the challenging task of notifying the victim's family. It was an arduous responsibility, but one that had to be done.

Chapter 15

Three Weeks Later . . .

Monk and Tangee returned from their vacation in Miami. Throughout their time away, Tangee had attempted to contact Shayla repeatedly, but to no avail. She couldn't call Cori or anyone else within their immediate circle who might have been able to connect her with Shayla. Eventually, she realized she needed to reach out to Shayla's mother to find out what was going on with her friend.

The coroner's office held Shayla's body two weeks leading up to that day. A thorough investigation was conducted prior to the family making preparations for the funeral. When Shayla's mother answered, her voice carried the weight of grief.

"Hello?" she said.

"Hey! Miss Judy. How are you? This is me, Tangela, Shay's friend. I've been trying to get in touch with her. Have you seen her around?" Tangee asked.

"Tangela, baby . . . Shay's dead. Somebody killed her about two weeks ago. We'll be having her funeral this Saturday, if you plan to be here," Shayla's mother informed with tears in her eyes and devastation evident in her voice, causing her words to catch in her throat.

Tangee's mouth fell open, her body stiffened. The phone slipped from her hand and clattered to the floor of Monk's palace, just atop the game room. She couldn't believe what she'd heard. Hastily, she collapsed onto the bed before she was to pass out, tears streaming down her face.

"Hello? Tangela. You there, baby? Speak to me," Shayla's mother, Miss Judy, called out through the phone.

Tangee remained on the bed, tears flowing uncontrollably. She was shattered by the news.

****

Hours Later . . .

Tangee awoke from the depressed nap she'd taken, finding Monk seated in the living room. She stumbled toward him, her legs still weak, her spirits lower than ever. Monk observed her unusual demeanor and saddened expression.

"You okay, sweetie?" he asked

"Monk . . . Shay's dead," she said somberly, collapsing onto the couch beside him.

"What?" he exclaimed.

"I said, my friend Shay. She's dead!" Tangee repeated, her voice heavy with grief.

"No! What happened? When did you find out?"

"Somebody killed her, Monk. Her mother told me earlier when I called."

"Damn! That's fucked up there. She didn't say what exactly happened?" Monk asked.

"No, but I'm about to go online and read the newspaper," Tangee said, then got back to her feet and went to the bedroom once more.

Monk was already aware of the hit Cold Heart had orchestrated to eliminate the problems Shayla presented. One hour after the fact, Cold Heart texted Monk and Body to let them know the job was done. He and the trigger man, Heem, were chilling at Cold Heart's mother's home, plotting their next move. Heem, once an ordinary young guy, had now become a teenage assassin. He was subject to being a force to be reckoned with.

Now that Shayla was dead, Monk knew he had to support Tangee through the grieving process and merely go through the motions. It was all part of the business. Murder was a part of street politics, and Drip held no qualms about eliminating anyone who impacted his bottom line: money. At the end of the day, this was all that mattered. Period.

Chapter 16

Hound Jr. and Lily met for lunch, finally having time alone since his return home. Lily had numerous thoughts she wanted to discuss with him. She sought clarity on the nature of their relationship and where they intended to take it. It was a Friday, and Lily had the weekend off.

They drove in Hound Jr.'s new Range Rover, on their way to an Italian restaurant in South Philly on 14th and Porter, owned by one of Angelo Marconi's nephews. Angelo was the Don over the Marconi crime family, and his youngest brother, Raphael, had a son named Carmine, who was around the same age as Hound Jr. They planned to discuss business related to the type of product Carmine had, a large scale supply of methamphetamine and various products produced there from. The two were already acquainted from previous encounters and aimed to establish a business connection.

"Nice ride you got here, Cornelius," Lily complimented his vehicle.

"Thank you," he responded with a smile, glancing over at her. "You like?"

"Oh yeah. Good choice. I love the color. It speaks volumes."

"Royal Blue. You already know it's my favorite color. But look. You say you wanted to talk over a few things of serious nature with me. I'm all ears. What's on your mind?" Hound Jr. asked of Lily.

She exhaled, gathering her thoughts. "Do you want me to begin with what I *want*, or what I *expected*?" she stated.

"Begin with what you expected. I don't wanna disappoint you by failing to live up to your expectations," he responded.

"Okay. Look, all the time you were gone, I held you down, Cornelius. I did everything you needed me to do. I safeguarded your money. I ran errands for you. I came to see you faithfully. I did everything a loyal woman is supposed to do for a man she has a son by and loves. Not to mention overlooking what you had going on with the many women when you were out here before. My expectations were that, when you came home, we were gonna get back together and really make something of what we had. That we was gonna get a home together, start a business, and truly make money together legitimately . . . as a married couple. But now that you're out, you want something totally different than I *thought* you would. Why is that?"

Lily laid out in plain language how she felt.

Hound Jr thought over her words. He had the proper response to them and wouldn't anger or disappoint Lily in the process.

"The reason I came out of prison the way I did is because, for one; I didn't want to rush myself into anything, especially with no female. I felt the need to explore my options. And to be honest, I don't know about that marriage thing. I ain't ready. Now, about us maintaining a solid friendship and going into business together, we can definitely do that. I ain't got no issue with that. Besides, I know you're tired of working for other people and ready to be your own boss—"

"I definitely am!" Lily quickly responded. "If only you knew. I've always questioned when will I be able to do the things I want to do and live the life I want to live. I want to turn this dream into a vision, Cornelius. And my vision into a reality. My realistic expectations are still in place. I simply gotta manifest them."

"You still got it in mind to do the modelling thing, start an upscale feminine clothing line, and own a ladies' boutique?" he asked her.

"And you know I do, Cornelius. You know who I always wanted to be. You know what I always wanted to do. And you know what? I feel like you *owe* that to me. I did tell you way back then that I'mma someday hold you to all those damn promises you made me back when we were strong. That day has come. And that time is now. I could've easily walked away on you with all your money, and begun the life I wanted for myself. But I didn't. I stayed down with you. And on top of that, the promise and potential that I'll someday have you all to myself weighed heavy on me. I wanted this. And then, you get out and do me like this. But it's okay. I'mma still be here for you. I couldn't care less about what you and that young girl got going on, Cornelius. You're *my* dude. Always have been and always will be."

Lily finally completed her long bottled-up words of emotions. A tear rolled down her cheek bone, adding an expression of raw feelings,

"How long you been hiding all that in, Lily? I need to know," Hound Jr. responded.

"Ever since the day they put you in cuffs and took you away from us. But for the most part, since the day I was in the labor room and our son came out of me," Lily stated.

"That was a day to remember, wasn't it? November twenty-first, nineteen ninety-one. My very first time seeing a baby born. My own child!"

She kept quiet, allowing the weight of her words to influence his feelings.

"A'ight, look, Lily. This is what we finna do. Okay. We will go into business together. I'mma put up all the money you need. And I'mma give you the freedom to lay out the blueprint how you see fit. We're gonna still be good friends, like we always have been. We gonna still do date night on

Thursdays, just like before. And all else you desire, we can still do. How does that sound?"

"Sounds like to me you left a few things out of that. You *owe* me, Cornelius. Big time. I made major sacrifices for you—all the way around. My body, my freedom, and my life. And now, it's my turn to cash in," she responded firmly.

"I understand that. But what part did I leave out?" he asked curiously.

"The part about me seeing you when *I* want to. The part about me having you when *I* want it. And, that part about us travelling and going on vacation together. *Those* parts," Lily stated, her lips pursed with a look of desire gracing her face as she pondered.

Hound Jr. couldn't help but smile at her words. It made him feel good to know he still held a strong sexual allure, but wasn't willing to give up his involvement with the young piece of pussy he had in Daniella, solely for Lily.

"Hey, if you wanna know, we're still able to do all that and more," he assured her, smiling. "But I'm not gonna give up what I've begun with my young *jawn,* to exclusively deal with you. That ain't gonna happen, Lily. On no accord. Now, what we could have happen is—I won't question you not one time about who you're dealing with or what you're doing, and in return, I expect you to give me that same respect. Deal?"

Lily looked on at him, smiled, and slowly nodded, acknowledging the arrangement he had proposed. She understood that she simply needed to play her part and eventually, he would come around. All she had to do was play her part—a task she found to be quite easy.

****

Hound Jr. and Lily arrived at the restaurant. In the days leading up to their meeting, Hound Jr. and Carmine reconnected through phone conversations and made plans to discuss business. The awaited moment had finally arrived.

Upon completing their lunch, Hound Jr. and Carmine took a walk up and down the block to discuss business matters. Meanwhile, Lily and Carmine's girlfriend—Marina—remained seated, engaging in their own conversation. Both Hound Jr. and Carmine told them to get used to it. That there will be many more days like that to come.

Carmine initiated discussions between him and his black business counterpart.

"So, you're ready to go back to business, huh, Cornelius? I know you've been itching to get things going again since you've found freedom."

"You already know, Carmine. I'm a hustla. Always have been. Always will be. But, I'm eager to learn about this new wave of high. I've heard so much about it, and can't wait to get my hands on a few bricks of it. When I was in Kentucky, I saw so much on the news, read so much about it, and heard good stories, that I decided meth would be my product of choice to make money from. It's more appealing than heroin. Both young and old love it, and you can take it with you anywhere you go, no matter the location. A customer is always available to buy a fix of meth. And pills can be pressed to include an added allure to make dough. I've heard from a few associates that the Italians got the hook-up on this, that your people hold the supply I'm after. I've got a couple dollars I want to invest. Tell me something good," Hound Jr. laid out his business proposal.

Carmine smiled as he listened to Hound Jr.'s enthusiasm. "Still the same eager and energetic Cornelius, I see. But to satisfy your inclinations, yeah, we've got it. The Italians are the gateway to the new drug every club in Philly is dying to have circulating in their environment. And I've got kilos of it. How much we talking about to begin this beautiful affair?" Carmine asked.

"I've got about three hundred grand. How many kilos will I get for that?" Hound Jr. inquired.

"Between twenty and thirty, depending. But the new shit I've gotten in from Amsterdam, the batch of pink material, is more potent than the white stuff, and it cost me a little more," Carmine explained.

"All I want is the best you got to offer. That's all that matters to me—having the best," Hound Jr. asserted.

"And the best is all I have to offer. Anything else would be uncivilized," Carmine responded.

The two men then turned to face each other, gripped hands tightly, and agreed to meet again, then they made their way back to the restaurant where the ladies were.

While strolling down the block, Lily got a call from Chloe. She had given birth to a baby boy the previous night, and wanted Lily to come to the hospital to see the baby and provide input on a name.

Fortunately, Von's parents were together when Chloe reached out. They both had the opportunity to be there for Chloe and Von at the same time. The grandparents made their way to the hospital to see the newborn baby.

****

Four Days Later . . .

Chloe and Baby Trevon Jr. were finally home from the hospital. Lily and Hound Jr. were eager to visit. This would be their second time seeing their grandchild within a week of being born, and they were thrilled. The two went out and bought gifts galore before the day and wanted to surprise Chloe with all they had.

Rosa was at home with Chloe as well, keeping to herself as she was due any day and wished to avoid activities that might trigger her water breaking. Hound Jr. knew nothing really about her involvement in the three-way relationship, let alone her pregnancy by Von also. All he knew was that his son had three girls pregnant at the same time. He would be in for a huge surprise.

Lily called Chloe to let her know they were outside the apartment. Chloe made her way to the door to let them in. Lily and Hound Jr. both exited Hound Jr's Range Rover and approached Chloe closely to greet her.

"Hello, Chloe! How are you, girl? You're already familiar with who Von's dad is," Lily said, embracing Chloe.

"Hi, Chloe! Nice to me you again," Hound Jr. said to her, also offering a hug.

"Nice to meet you again as well."

"Now where's that grand boy of ours? We're ready to see him. We brought a lot of gifts for him too. Everything's out in the truck," Lily informed Chloe as they entered the apartment.

Rosa was seated on the couch, smiling at their company. Lily noticed her first.

"Hey!" she greeted.

"Hello!" Rosa responded.

"Didn't know you had company, Chloe," Lily said, turning her head and speaking to her.

"I don't, Miss Lily. We live together now."

"Oh! I see she's almost due herself."

"Mmm-hmm! And that's the reason why we're glad the both of you are here together. Vonnie's mom and dad and me and Rosa. And as for you sir, we have something to share with you, if Miss Lily haven't mentioned it already?" Chloe informed.

Lily and Hound Jr. took a seat, preparing to hear what the young ladies were about to reveal to him. Lily already knew but allowed the girls the chance to relate their reality to him themselves.

Lily smiled delightfully, her hands resting gracefully atop one another on her knee, legs crossed in an elegant manner.

"I know what y'all about to say. But go ahead and let Cornelius know. I don't want him to speculate any longer. So go ahead and give him the details."

Hound Jr. chuckled softly, recognizing how much Chloe's approach resembled Lily's own. Lily glanced at him and mirrored his amusement.

Chloe and Rosa exchanged amusing smiles before Chloe proceeded with what she had to say.

"Me and—"

"I'm pregnant by Vonnie too, Mister," Rosa interjected, unable to contain herself.

"Why'd you have to spoil it for me, Rosa?" Chloe teased, though her tone was playful.

"You was taking too long, boo. I was ready to see his reaction to the news of our lifestyle," Rosa responded. "And also, sir, I'm the one Vonnie was with one day when you called and y'all had a conversation. If you may recall?"

"Hold up. Wait a minute. You and Rosa are related? And, the both of you are involved with my son. He must really be a special dude to you both," Hound Jr. remarked.

"He was simply too good for either of us to let go off once the truth came to the light. So the three of us just agreed to be with each other and got a place to live together. No harm, no foul, no sneaking around," Chloe explained, looking back and forth between Lily and Hound Jr.

"Just that simple," remarked Lily.

"Well . . . the truth is aways stranger than fiction, in most cases, Miss Lily," Rosa stated.

"And our only job is to not complicate it, but to enjoy it to the best of our ability," Chloe chimed in, echoing Rosa's positivism.

They continued to talk, each side becoming more familiar with the other. Lily and Hound Jr. were drawn in, eager to hear the interesting story Chloe and Rosa had to tell. She never really knew everything.

Chapter 17

One Month Later . . .

Jeffery Toliver, the friend of both Von and Cold Heart, was granted a reasonable bail by the Federal Judge presiding over his case. His cooperation and willingness to assist both the federal and state government in their investigations, particularly regarding a shooting death he witnessed first-hand, earned JT leniency, allowing him to await trial as a free man.

He and the mother of his daughter shared a residence in South Philly on 21st Street. JT still possessed money he'd saved from his brief stint when Von provided him with opportunities, including running operations at the spot on 8th and Diamond, a territory once fortified by Tobias.

Cold Heart had yet to collect the debt JT owed Von and was now intent on doing so. Knowing the whereabouts of JT's mother's home, Cold Heart saw it as a starting point. Instead of directly approaching the house and inquiring about JT's location, Cold Heart opted to go about things in a different approach. He parked his car discreetly nearby, keeping watch for two consecutive nights, patiently awaiting a sighting of either JT himself or his girlfriend, Creshonda, whom he also knew by sight.

Finally, there was some activity. Creshonda stopped by JT's mother's house, ostensibly to pick up their daughter, driving the Buick Lacrosse provided by JT, a light brown vehicle Cold Heart was familiar with from previous encounters with JT and Von. Now, all he needed to do was tail her to their residence, hoping to catch JT unaware, or to await his arrival. The plan was to grab hold of Creshonda and their daughter, then make JT come to him. With Heem by his side, Cold Heart was prepared for any resistance JT might offer.

Cold Heart trailed Creshonda from North Philly to their place in South Philly. He allowed her enough time to get out the car, unbuckle the three-year-old from the seat, and make way to the front door. Meanwhile, Heem, Cold Heart's accomplice, exited the vehicle, already briefed on their plan. Cold Heart circled the block and parked on the adjacent street.

Creshonda settled the little girl on the doorstep so to open the door. The November chill bit into the night air, urging her to hasten her movements. She swiftly managed to unlock the door and was about to bend down to lift her daughter once more when Heem rushed forward, forcefully pushing Creshonda to the living room floor of the house. With a swift motion, Heem brandished his weapon, a heavy Colt .45 pistol glinting ominously in the dim light.

Whop!

Heem smacked her hard across the head with the banger, then trained the gun on her as if about to shoot. He then grabbed the little girl by the arm to bring her inside and eased the door up, awaiting Cold Heart to show. The young madman then tied up Creshonda. Moments later, Cold Heart was there. They secured the door and conducted a thorough search of the house to ensure no one else was present before dragging Creshonda upstairs to the bedroom.

"Bitch, where the fuck that nut-ass nigga you got for a boyfriend?" Cold Heart barked at her.

"Fuck you, pussy! Find him if you want him!"

"What!" Heem spat.

Whop!

Heem smacked her again.

Whop!

And again.

"You wanna continue to play tough, bitch! I bet if we keep smacking your ass around, you'll tell us what we want to know then, now won't you?"

Whop!

"Won't you?"

With a final flurry, Heem grasped the pistol by the barrel and struck her across the face with the handle multiple times, nearly rendering her unconscious throughout the ordeal. Creshonda's wrists were already bound, and there was nothing she could truly do to block out clear blows.

Cold Heart and Heem lifted her and flung her onto the bed, positioning her on her belly, her head hanging off the mattress. Blood seeped from the wounds inflicted by the vicious blows down to the floor, staining the carpet drop by drop.

Cold Heart then picked up the little girl and sat her down at the edge of the bed next to her mother. He then grabbed Creshonda's cell phone from her purse.

"What's the code to unlock this shit, bitch?"

Her face had swollen so bad she could barely talk or see.

Whop!

"Speak up!" Heem barked at her this time.

"Why are you doing this to me? I ain't got nothing do with who JT told on when they locked him up."

Both Cold Heart and Heem furrowed their eyebrows and exchanged puzzled glances at the revelation.

"When did they lock him up?" Cold Heart inquired, intrigued.

"Months ago. He's been out on bail since."

"And when is that nigga supposed to be coming home to you?"

"He don't tell me nothing. JT just shows up whenever he wants."

"And where he hustle at now? Where he got the product hid at? Where's the money, bitch?" Cold Heart drilled.

"You can find whatever you might be looking for over there in that closet," Creshonda said to him.

"Check that out, bro," Cold Heart said to Heem.

Heem darted to the closet, flung it open, and rummaged through it for valuables. There, hidden away, he found only money—a total of $25,000 tucked neatly in a shoebox. He presented it to Cold Heart.

"I found this in the sneaker box."

"Cool. Count it up and see what we got," Cold Heart said to Heem, then placed his attention back on Creshonda. "What's the pass-code to this phone, bitch?" he growled.

She disclosed it. Cold Heart unlocked it and began scanning the contacts, halting at JT's name.

"We 'bout to call JT and let him know we got you and the daughter. Go get the car, bro. It's around the block. Better yet, why don't we load her and the kid into her car and hold them until he shows up with the rest of that money! Once we've got him in our hands, we'll beat the truth out of him until he spills on everyone he's snitched on," Cold Heart declared.

Heem seized Creshonda's car keys and dashed downstairs and out the door to open the doors and trunk. He made it back to Cold Heart and they both gripped her by the arms and legs, then hauled her to the trunk. They put the little girl in the back seat. Heem would do the driving. Cold Heart went around the block to go to his car, and they planned to reconvene at his discreet hideout—the same location where he and Fat Steve whacked Meatball and Ill-Will.

****

One Hour Later . . .

Creshonda lay tightly bound and gagged on the bedroom floor, while the little girl slumbered on the sofa chair nearby.

"We bout to call this nigga, JT, now, bitch!" Cold Heart spat. "Rip that bitch clothes off, bro. We gonna take a picture and send to him to show him we mean business."

Heem proceeded to tear the thin fabric from Creshonda's body, leaving her exposed. Cold Heart snapped three photos before moving to the living room to capture images of the little girl. He sent them to JT from Creshonda's phone and awaited him to call. He did so within thirty seconds.

Cold Heart answered the call. "Now that you know we ain't playing no games . . . where that paper at you owe Vonnie, nigga!"

"Yo, who the fuck you be!" JT responded.

"Stop playing, nigga! You know who I am! Now, where's the rest of that cash? Or I will get ruthless!"

JT hesitated. He also recognized the voice.

"And I know bro spotted you two bricks. That's every bit of eighty grand. We got the twenty-five out your bitch crib. You owe *fiddy-five* more. Where is it? Don't let your baby mom and little girl die behind some shit you got going on. And I believe you the one who supposed to be ratting on bro about that shit to happen when dude banged his ride. I know you were there. Don't forget, nigga. He called me when that happened. I'm the one who dropped you off at your mom's house. How you think I knew how to track you down? I knew your mom always baby-sit for you and your girl. All I had to do was follow her from there to your spot to track you down. You wasn't there, so we grabbed them. Now you got two choices: Come up with the cash you owe; or be forced to bury them both if you don't!" Cold Heart spat, then promptly hit the button to end the call.

JT hurried to call him back to make a compromise. He spoke in a panic. "Listen, Cold, please don't hurt my girl and our baby. I'm begging you, bro. I'll hustle up the money. I don't have it yet. I got busted by the feds and had to bail myself out. Just give me some time.".

"So, you did get busted? What charges did they slap you with?"

"Some work and those hammers I bought from you," JT responded. He spoke loose and recklessly. Like he was recording the call.

"And how the fuck you get out? Who did you rat on?"

"I didn't snitch on anyone, bro. I lied to 'em. I had to trick 'em."

"What the fuck you mean by that?"

"There was two dick head detectives from Philly Homicide that approached me when the feds took me in. Some nigga name Bill Hilliard, and his partner, a Spanish cat name Valente Canelo." JT had a solid memory and was eager to recall. "They grilled me about Vonnie, claiming they had a witness who saw him take someone out. I didn't say anything. But, I did notice Tobias's car around that day, the guy whose turf we took over after Vonnie had that incident. I saw his car in the area a few times afterward too."

"Who the fuck is Tobias?" Cold Heart inquired, although he already had an inkling from Von making him aware.

"He's Tobias Flowers. Dude drives a gray colored Benz. Or maybe it was smoke-black," JT clarified. "A Beamer I meant. Sorry about that."

"Check that. Understood. But, why the fuck they came to you if you ain't have nothing to tell 'em? Something doesn't add up, JT. But back to business. Where that money at, nigga?"

"You gotta give me some time, Cold. I'mma have it. Just give me some time," JT pleaded.

Cold Heart pulled out his Desert Eagle fifty caliber pistol, cocked it, then paused to speak once more.

"Please, JT! This man is gonna kill us if you don't give him their money!" Creshonda managed to cry out through the gag, still lying chest down on the bed.

"Give you some time, huh? Three-two-one! Time's up, nigga!" Cold Heart declared, then rammed the barrel of the gun into Creshonda's backside and pulled the trigger.

Bang!

Blood splattered, following a deafening blast. A thick glob of blood coated the pistol.

Bang!

Heem aimed at her head and fired his gun, ending her life instantly.

Bang!

A final round by Cold Heart concluded the execution.

"Noooooo!" JT's voice rang out through the phone.

Cold Heart terminated the call and removed the battery from Creshonda's phone to prevent further tracking. They then wrapped her body in a rug. He used her shirt to wipe the blood from the gun, and loaded her into the trunk of her car. The little girl would be spared. Cold Heart planned to drop her off at JT's mother's house. He would knock loudly to get her attention, then quickly flee the scene. He lastly intended to set Creshonda's car ablaze with her body inside.

The next step from there was to locate JT and deal with him regarding everything as well. There was a concern that he might run to the feds for certain now and divulge everything he knew about Cold Heart, Von, and the crew. With time ticking away, everyone was on a tight deadline. The question loomed: Who would meet their inevitable ending first?

Chapter 18

September 2009
Two Months Earlier . . .
The hitter who'd taken aim inside *The Ozone* and shot three people, then executed a daring escape from the scene, made it to his designated location safely. His getaway vehicle awaited him two blocks around the corner, driven by his cousin, a guy named Polo. They were now ready to return to their hometown of Pittsburgh.

"Go-go-go!" shouted the twenty-four-year-old known as "Tank." He was the assailant.

"Did you get him? The nigga Drip! Did you hit him?" Polo inquired of his younger cousin.

"I know I hit somebody. Two or three people to be exact!" Tank said.

"We didn't have instructions to hit *two or three* other people, Tank. Brazy said specifically to pop that nigga Drip. But we'll know what's up at some point soon. The homie, Rolla, gonna call and let us know what's up sometime tonight or tomorrow. But we gotta get back to Pittsburgh now. Let me call Brazy and update him," said Polo, pulling out his phone to contact his big homie.

The beef between the person who ordered the hit (Brazy) on Drip started months prior to the shooting. It originated from a Super Bowl party at a popular sports bar in Atlantic City, when the Pittsburgh Steelers played the Arizona Cardinals. Brazy, a Pittsburgh native, supported the home team, while Drip rooted for the Arizona Cardinals. They put $200K on the game, and when the Steelers won, Drip bucked on paying the debt, disrespecting Brazy in front of witnesses. Enraged, Brazy had to retaliate, and he did so with force, by sending his young protégé to take him out. It was the only clear opportunity they would have to eliminate Drip, whose movements were unpredictable and shrouded in secrecy.

Before the Super Bowl incident, Drip and Brazy were acquainted through business dealings. Brazy had purchased four bricks of heroin from Drip, introduced by Rolla, a Philadelphia native Bishop Blood gang member familiar with Drip from their neighborhood.

Brazy had intended to buy more product from Drip the same day of the bet but deemed it unnecessary after the Steelers' victory. Drip unknowingly thwarted Brazy's plans, unwittingly making an enemy. From February to September, Brazy meticulously plotted his revenge, making Drip believe he was safe until he sent Tank to carry out the hit. Rolla, present at the club as well, directed Tank to take the shot at the opportune moment.

****

November 2009
Presently ...

The investigation into the shooting at *The Ozone* was concluded and the sixty-day restriction was lifted, allowing Drip to resume business. He took proactive measures to enhance security by installing a high-tech metal detector at the entrance, and all bouncers now carry wands for random checks.

Despite the resolution, the shooting continued to weigh heavily on Drip's mind

Who the fuck felt like they were that tough to come into my shit and take shots at me and my people? he thought to himself as he sat behind the desk in his office there in *The*

Ozone, preparing to review the shooting footage one more time.

With Body and Animal by his side, Drip planned to reopen on Thanksgiving night, just a few days away.

"Whoever the motherfucka was, he had to have a pair of tough nuts on him. We was moving in on him, then, he made that Hollywood ass stunt on us," remarked Animal, cracking his knuckles. "If it wasn't for that, we would've had his ass."

As they reviewed the tape, Body noticed something peculiar about the shooter's appearance. "Pause and zoom in on his face," he instructed Drip. Drip complied.

Body pointed out a distinctive flame tattoo on the shooter's throat. "Take a look at his throat, Drip. Look at the flame tattoo. The colorful ink to it."

"Yeah. What about it?" Drip responded.

"You know I have a solid memory, bro. I can never lose that ability while in my line of work. And if my memory serves me well, ain't that the same young nigga who was with that fool, Brazy, out in AC? The one involved in that deal with you?" Body recalled.

Drip's interest piqued as he recognized the ink scars.

"Motherfuckin' right it is! That bitch-ass nigga, Brazy! He's the one who was behind that shit!"

"But I don't recall seeing Brazy himself that night!" Animal interjected.

"Come to think of it, I do remember seeing Rolla there though. He's the one who introduced me to Brazy," Drip remembered.

"But why would Brazy send a hitter at us like that? We don't bang! He a blood nigga, ain't he?" asked Body.

"Because I told that pussy *fuck him* on that paper behind that bet on the Super bowl. He shouldn't have been popping all that shit! Tryna put on for them bitches in the bar and whatnot!" Drip said.

"So the nigga built up his nuts to send somebody to take aim at you, thinking shit was sweet!" Body surmised.

"Apparently so," remarked Drip. "And now we gonna smack that pussy back in the worst way. We gonna smash him and everyone close to him once we run down on that fuck! But in the meantime, we gonna find that nigga Rolla, and have him lead us straight to the fool. I've got the perfect plot in mind too. Don't forget, we know Rolla from around our hood. And know where his grandparents live. And, I was wondering why he or that nigga Brazy didn't never get back at me about buying more work after the fact. Now I know why. He was guilty of something." Drip vented his frustrations

"What's the plan then?" Body inquired.

Drip laid out his strategy. Both Body and Animal agreed that it was the best course of action. Something needed to be done to prevent another attempted hit from Brazy, and Drip's plan seemed promising.

****

Hound Jr. made it a priority to spend time with Kidada's mom, Juanita, something he hadn't done since the day after his release when he retrieved the money she had been holding for him. The other half of which she had wisely put away in the bank.

His plan for the day was to take Juanita out to lunch, followed by an occasion to go jewelry shopping (knowing she adored rose gold), and to discuss the status of their relationship.

Juanita, with her more outgoing personality compared to Lily, was unapologetically forthright and assertive. She had no qualms about speaking her mind, regardless of the consequences. Her words flowed freely, unfiltered, reflecting her true self. However, her intentions were never malicious, provided no harm was intended or taken.

They set out in Hound Jr.'s impeccably clean truck. He had a penchant for keeping his vehicles spotless, and his

Range Rover had received a $200 detailing earlier that morning.

"So what's your plan, Cornelius? I know you've got something cooking. Just clue me in, am I part of it?" Juanita asked as they drove.

"I got a little something churning. Don't wanna reveal anything until the proper time, but first, I gotta be sure I do all I can for my boy, to help him outta the situation he is in," he responded.

"Damn! That's right. I forgot about Vonnie and what he's going through. How is he?"

"He's holding up. Hopefully, they'll drop the charges soon; they don't have much on him," Hound Jr. answered.

"That's a relief. I've seen bits about him and Lily in the news and papers. Kidada keeps me informed, but you know how secretive she can be," Juanita remarked.

"My baby just how I want her to be," Hound Jr. said proudly.

"She definitely is. That girl didn't tell me a thing about you getting out."

"That's because I told her not to say anything to anybody."

"Well, she didn't. Not even to me, her Momma."

"That's Daddy's girl. To do things exactly like I say and how I tell her to," Hound Jr. remarked.

His cell phone vibrated. He pulled it from the clip on his belt. It was Cold Heart calling.

"Yeah, what's good, Cold?" he answered.

"I'm coolin', O.G. I got some important information we could use to help Vonnie out of this situation."

"Oh yeah. Like what?"

"I'mma go ahead and talk over the phone. I know your line not a hot hit. You just got that phone."

"Right. But talk to me. What you got?" Hound Jr. urged him on.

"Vonnie got at me, and told me to go collect a heavy debt from some dude we knew owe him. I wasn't able to find that nigga, but, I found his girl, then me and one of my people mounted pressure on her to cough up the goods. We called him on her phone. He had no choice but to tell us what we wanted to know. We had the baby-momma and the baby."

"What about the paper?"

"I was getting to that part. The nigga claim he didn't have it. And he needed time. Basically trying to bullshit me. I don't play no games. We put the pressure down more on his bitch. Then he gave me the run down on everything . . ."

Cold Heart related the whole exchange of words between him and JT. He then gave Hound Jr. the names of the two detectives investigating the one homicide JT knew of.

"Look, you ain't got too much going on later, do you?" Hound Jr. asked.

"Nah. We might be able to link up later. I gotta swing by Lily's house to meet her anyway. I got a few dollars of Vonnie to drop off."

"Okay. That'll work. I'll hit you up. We all can talk together."

"No doubt, O.G."

The call ended.

Returning his attention to Juanita, Hound Jr. explained, "As the mother of my only daughter, Juanita, you're inevitably part of my plans."

Juanita, seizing the moment, asserted, "Then I expect to have more say in things than Lily, right?"

Hound Jr. chuckled at her remark. "You haven't lost your edge, Juanita."

"I surely haven't. And I don't plan to let any other woman get ahead of me when it comes to a man who's mine," she retorted. "While you were away, I used to think over how you played between me and Lily. She caught us together a time or two and I caught you both together the same way," Juanita added.

"And 'Lady Justice' had more game than the both of you. She held me down strong for eleven years. But anyway, where you wanna have lunch? What you got in mind?"

"Let's hit *Red Robins*. I ain't been there in a while," Juanita responded.

"I ain't been there ever. Where one at?"

Juanita suggested a location in Bucks County. "You know I've gotta place up in Bucks County, right?"

"Oh you do?" Juanita exclaimed, intrigued by the coincidence.

"Mm-hmm."

"I'm interested in learning more about the young woman you've got in your life. Kiki mentioned her to me, saying they're around the same age," said Juanita.

As Hound Jr. delved into the details of his acquaintance with Daniella, Juanita couldn't help but feel a pang of jealousy and envy. Despite this, she knew she couldn't openly challenge the situation or engage in the potential confrontation she had in mind regarding Hound Jr.'s attention.

With more experience than Daniella and strong sense of self-image, Juanita understood that Hound Jr. wouldn't prioritize her over the younger woman in his life no way. Therefore, she resolved to simply let him have his way as he pleased, without disrupting the peace he cherished.

****

They arrived at the restaurant, enjoyed their meal, and then proceeded with their day.

"Okay, so now what? I'm in the mood for a little shopping. I need a few new pieces of jewelry. And you owe me for keeping it real with you, Cornelius. It's time for my reward," Juanita said.

"I had that on the agenda. I know what you like. And yes, I'm gonna reward you, Juanita," he responded with a smile. "You deserve it. I do owe you."

"That's good to know. And I'm hoping this is gonna be an all-day affair. I'm trying to have you fuck me real good later, if this be in the agenda as well?" she let out with a smile. "I ain't had none of that dick of yours in years. And I want it," she expressed in her own special way.

He smiled in response, showing teeth. "We can do that too. Juanita. I've always liked being with you sexually," he said, chewing on gum as he navigated his truck through the busy streets.

They went shopping down-town Center City Philly. Juanita was treated to a diamond necklace, diamond-studded earrings, and a matching bracelet. He steered clear from buying her a ring, not wanting to send the wrong message or have her entertain misconceptions about their relationship. It was only a friendship. Nothing more.

Later, they then rented a hotel suite and fucked like they were young all over again. Those feelings Juanita had reserved for him returned. She could potentially be a problem for him with emotions playing a part. Therefore, he needed to proceed with caution with her, especially considering the line of business he was looking to involve himself in. Any time a man has to deal with the feelings and emotions of a woman who had a feisty attitude like Juanita, he was playing with fire. Not a good thing.

Chapter 19

Monyetta, Kidada, Tiona, and Ayonna seemed to have formed a stronger bond after the shooting at *The Ozone*, whether through familial ties or relationships within their circle. It seemed natural to them to form a sisterhood, establish businesses, and forge a future together. Ayonna had healed well from the gunshot wound to her inner thigh, the bullet narrowly missing the bone as it passed through.

On this particular Saturday, Monyetta and Kidada met up with Ayonna at her place, intending to go shopping at the *Franklin Mills Mall*, *The Gallery Mall*, and *The Cherry Hill Mall*, making it a girls' day out. As they arrived at Ayonna's apartments, Monk was there chilling with his girl, planning to watch college football all day. It was eleven in the morning.

"Hey, girls!" Ayonna greeted.

"Hey, girl!" responded Monyetta, her lifelong friend.

"Hey, 'Yonna," Kidada said.

After exchanging greetings, they all hugged and kissed before stepping inside.

"Oh shit! What's good, fam?" Kidada greeted Monk.

"Hey, Kiki! How you doing? What's the deal on Vonnie?" Monk responded, getting to his feet to hug his cousin.

"I'm good, fam. And bro, he's been holding it down like a real G. It shouldn't be too much longer before his first court appearance. He's definitely good now, being that pops is out and is able to take care of everything," Kidada replied.

"No doubt. We definitely gonna see to it that all is well. Because we gonna be sure it ends well. You feel me?" Monk stated.

"And you know I do, fam," responded Kidada.

"Monk, let me speak with you for a moment, please sweetie," Ayonna said, leading him to their room to talk. Ayonna also needed to get dressed, having already taken care of her hair, lashes, make-up, and lip gloss.

"I'm low on money, baby. I need a few dollars to go shopping, please," she asked Monk.

Monk went to the stash in the closet and pulled out a few stacks of cash. Counting $4,000, he handed it to her.

"Don't forget, Ayonna, I'm trying to save so I can buy a home. That's my ultimate plan, to buy me a home at some point in the future. Let's keep that in mind. A'ight?" he said to her.

The precision of his words left Ayonna feeling jaded. It was not just *what* he said, but also *how* he said it. *He's trying to save so he can buy himself a home, huh? That's what his ultimate plan is. No 'me' in that, I see*, Ayonna thought, catching the underlying intent behind his statement.

Ayonna was tempted to push back on the subtle remark, but did not want to spoil the mood. Maybe the time wasn't right for her to let him know that she was pregnant, that they had a baby on the way.

"I understand, Monk. I don't plan to spend your money like I don't have any sense," she said, accepting the money he held out for her.

They kissed before Monk returned to the living room to lock in on the football game that was about to begin. Meanwhile, Ayonna got dressed. Once she was ready, she headed towards the front of the house, and then she and her girls left, embarking on their shopping trip as they had planned.

****

While out shopping at the Gallery Mall, the girls engaged in a deep conversation about their career aspirations.

"Kidada, as the trendsetter of our group, what are thinking of pursuing in terms of business?" Ayonna inquired.

Monyetta already had a sense of Kidada's interests.

"I'm not entirely sure yet. I need to explore my strengths and see where I can make a profit. My dad mentioned owning a club or a bar in the night-life scene, so I might explore that avenue. But honestly, I'm open to anything," Kidada responded. "What about you, 'Yonna? Any plans?"

"I see myself getting into the health and beauty care industry, particularly focusing on products like hair extensions, lashes, and skincare products, tailored to the needs of Black consumers," Ayonna replied.

The conversation prompted them to reflect on their expenditures on beauty products, realizing the substantial market potential. "I never considered how much money we contribute to these industries annually. It's definitely worth considering as a business opportunity," Monyetta remarked.

Unlike her girlfriends, Monyetta had savings stashed away for her future plans, including investing in education. However, unexpected legal troubles loomed for her partner, Von. Nonetheless, he knew his money was in good hands.

Monyetta proposed pooling their resources, she and her sister Tiona, to invest in businesses aligned with their spending habits. "We can leverage our collective funds to start a business together. I'm about to graduate and pursue a career in journalism, so I'll have stable income soon," she suggested.

"So we're gonna see you on TV every day?" Kidada asked.

"Y'all sure would. And I can't wait. But while I'm on the air, y'all can be selling the products we're gonna have for sale. But we're gonna have to come together and agree on going into business together. How y'all feel about this?" Monyetta stated.

"Fuck it. I'm in. I ain't got too much else going on. And I know I can get all the money I need from my Pop," Kidada said. "He'll support me to the fullest on something like this."

"I'm in too," Ayonna said. "But I've got something else to put my attention on at the present time. I'm pregnant. And Kidada, I know Monk is close to you and he's your people and all. But I ask that you please don't say anything to him about what I'm sharing with y'all. Okay?"

"That's not my place to do women like that, 'Yonna. I'm not that type of female. I stay in my place. I stay in my lane!" Kidada said.

"Good. I'm glad to know I can trust you. But exactly when do y'all wanna come together and get this business plan rolling?" Ayonna asked.

"We can do that next weekend. By that time, I'm sure we'll have the money in place and begin laying out the business plan to what we're looking to get into," Monyetta said.

"For sho," Kidada said. "But in the meantime, look at these pretty-ass heels here. These bitches gonna look good on my feet. What y'all think?"

The girls continued shopping, bonding over their friendship and aspirations. Tiona wasn't able to make it. She and Cold Heart were preoccupied somewhere else. Despite Tiona's absence, the girls remained focused on their bond and the potential of their friendship to strengthen through their business venture.

****

It didn't take JT long to realize that his girlfriend had been killed. That Cold Heart's actions weren't a hoax. He'd heard the gunshot, the final scream of Creshonda, and the seriousness in Cold Heart's words.

Rushing to his girlfriend's house to check on her and their baby, he had to change routes. His mother called him to let him know that someone had dropped off his daughter, banged on the door, and disappeared before she'd gotten to the front to see who it was.

Noticing Creshonda's car missing, JT panicked and rushed to his mother's home from their place. Relieved to find his daughter safe, but still distraught over the girlfriend, he contacted Bill Hilliard, whose number he had, to report the incident with Creshonda and the danger he was now in. He was hell-bent on requesting protection. Bill and Valco, tired after a long day at work, had just returned home when they received JT's call, forcing them to head back to address the issue presented by the confidential informant.

Upon their return, JT was already in tears and visibly distraught in the interview room.

"What's the problem, Mister Toliver? What was your issue?" Bill asked.

"Please! You gotta help me. He killed my daughter's mom, sir," JT said in a fit of panic.

"Wait-wait-wait! Calm down. Who killed your daughter's mom?"

"Eunice did."

"Eunice! Who's he?"

"He's the friend of the Savage boy. He kidnapped her and then took her life."

"How do you know that? And why was she a target—Your daughter's mother?"

"He called me about money I owed the Savage dude. I told him I don't have it because I'd got locked up with the product I was fronted. That I need time to come up with the money. I was basically trying to put him off long enough so I can run here to y'all for protection. I didn't make it in time," JT stated

Curious, Valco wrote down all JT had to say. He also turned on an audio recorder and sat on the table as JT continued to reveal details. He explained his connection to Von and Cold Heart, starting from their altercation that the Lassiter guy had with Von over the car incident. JT divulged their history of growing up together, their involvement in the heroin trade, and the notorious activities of Von's Savage family. Bill and Valco took note, realizing the significance of the information provided. They planned to further investigate the names JT mentioned, so to build their case more strongly against Von.

As for JT, he faced a dilemma. Seeking witness protection would mean forfeiting his bail and going into custody, which he was unwilling to do. His only recourse was to rely on calling the police in emergencies or reaching out to Bill and Valco to supplement his previous statements. These were the limited options he had left.

Chapter 20

Drip, Body, and Animal, all took a ride from *The Ozone* to the home of Ahmad Saunders' grandparents. Known as "Rolla" in the streets, Ahmad was a member of the Bishop Blood Set.

Upon arrival, Drip knocked on the door and was met by the elderly lady who owned the place. "May I help you, gentlemen?" she asked.

The grandparents raised Rolla since he was a little boy. His mom was a horrible dope head, and his dad had never been around.

"Miss Virginia. Hey! How are you doing? It's me. Damien. Ahmad's friend. Do you remember me?" Drip stated.

"I think I do. Refresh my memory?"

"I'm Mickey Savage's grandson. Ahmad used to stay the night with me and my cousins at my grandparents' house. He went to school with us too."

"Yeah, baby. I remember you now." The old lady smiled. "How may I help you?"

"I'm trying to get in touch with Ahmad. He around?"

"No. Can I take a message for him?"

"I really need to speak with him in person. I've got some money I owe him."

"Well, as much as me and my husband done did for that boy, you can just give that money to me, and we ain't gotta say too much of nothing to him about it, baby," Mrs. Virginia responded with a chuckle and a smile.

"I ain't got no problem with doing that," Drip let out, now smiling himself. He pulled out a roll of money and peeled off ten $100 bills, then passed to her.

"Here you go. May we come inside, have you call him, and we can wait on him to come over?" Drip asked.

"You gentlemen definitely can," she said, and was delighted to let them in with no problem.

The money caused her to lower her guard. Also, with the mentioning of his grandfather's name, Drip made her feel good about his presence at her home.

The three of them went inside. They took seats in the living room. Mrs. Virginia then called her grandson to inform him of their visit and the money.

Rolla was so anxious to know who the guys was, he missed the name that his grandma mentioned. The time was five in the afternoon. Rolla was fifteen minutes away at his girlfriend's house in West Philly. He got into his car and headed to his grandparents' house.

Upon arrival, Rolla noticed a clean Range Rover parked outside, but saw no immediate threat. He tucked his gun under the seat of the car, got out and walked to the front door. Once he entered, he stopped dead in his tracks at the sight of Drip and his two cohorts. Rolla was paralyzed out of fear. Drip flashed him a grin.

"What's good, Rolla?" said Drip. "How you been, my brother?"

Rolla's grandmother then spoke. "This young man has been real nice to me, Ahmad. It's a blessing for you to have a friend like him," the old lady uttered, then flashed the money Drip had given her.

Rolla was still at a loss for words.

"I'mma leave you boys in here and let y'all talk over the business. Your friend means well, Ahmad. Anybody who come to find you when they got money to pay, they definitely mean good." Mrs. Virginia then walked to the den area of the house where her husband was watching TV.

"Drip," Rolla finally uttered.

"And you know it, Rolla. You gotta know I was smart enough to figure that shit out with what happened. Me and you grew up together. You must've forgot. And we kinda sorta know how each other think. But the best part about this is . . . I came to see you in peace. As you can see," he said, pointing in the direction of the grandparents—a silent code to indicate he let them live.

"You came in peace, you say. Well, why you didn't come by yourself?"

"Because, I didn't want you to take my presence out of context. My two homies here are more out of caution and protection than anything. They came in peace as well, but let's get to the real part . . . why we're here. I wanna make you a proposition. We already know everything about who gave the order to come shoot. I put it all together. When your blood gang brother—Brazy—never showed back up to buy more product from me, and then somebody all of a sudden show up at my bar grand opening and began blasting in the direction where I stood, I knew what was up then. It took a minute, but I put it together."

Rolla listened attentively, observing Body and Animal to be sure they weren't about to draw down on him with guns. They were cooling and not posing a threat.

"What you want from me?" Rolla asked.

"Like I said, I've got a business proposition for you. You're my homie. From childhood. You from Philly. *Not* Pittsburgh. Philly niggaz stick together no matter who or what!" Drip said.

"And your point?"

Drip shrugged before responding. "Don't nothing beat the cross but the double-cross, you feel me?"

"What that supposed to mean?"

"It means, I had three of my people get hit that night. I lost out on a lot of money because I had to shut down my bar. Me and my people had to go through so much behind that attempted hit on me. Not to mention one of my cousins nearly lost his life. Then had to go to jail on some unrelated shit. Brazy took us through all that because he and I had a beef. I'm the one who reneged on paying the money from the bet we made on the Super Bowl. He should have confronted me about it directly. But he didn't," Drip stated.

"And what you looking for me to do?" Rolla asked emphatically.

"Let me tell you what I've got to offer first, then, I'll let you know what I want you to do. How does that sound?"

"Hit me with it."

"A'ight, listen, I've got fifty bands for you off the rip. In addition to that, I'mma let you have one of the North Philly spots I got, or one of my upstate locations, to hustle and get money. Then, I'mma set you up and supply you with all the work you need. You ain't got to pay nothing. All I want you to do is, lead that nigga Brazy and the one who pulled the trigger, here to Philly, and put that nigga down right there where he be. Then the other one too."

Rolla thought over the proposition offered. He came to the conclusion that he really didn't have much of a choice. Truth be told, Drip could've easily killed his grandparents and him if he had wanted to. But he spared them. For whatever reason. Rolla knew it wasn't likely that Drip would show the same mercy twice. Not to mention the money he could make and the position he would be placed in to kill a fellow gang member and another. Two out-of-town niggaz he really didn't know like he knew Drip. He conveyed his decision.

"You got me in a tough situation, Drip. No lie. You always knew how to pull off a power move. A real slick-ass nigga, I tell you. I guess I ain't got no choice. You could've come my way with guns up, taken out grandma and grandpa. But you didn't. You showed mercy. And I guess I ain't got no choice," Rolla said.

Drip, Body, and Animal all nodded that he was in agreement to everything Rolla stated. It could have been much worse. Drip chose diplomacy over mayhem. And at the end of the day, that was the best thing to do.

"When do I get paid?" Rolla asked.

"The moment you let me know you're all in," responded Drip.

"Fuck it! I'm in. I'll do it. But I don't want to be the one to take them out. Y'all gotta do that."

"We ain't got no problem with that," Body chimed in.

That was his department in Drip's organization: to serve and protect, to do what Drip needed him to do, and to protect him from danger.

Drip and the boys got to their feet at that point. He then dug into his pocket and pulled out the roll of money he had.

"Call your grandma back in here, Rolla," Drip said to him.

"Nana! Let me see you in the living room again please!"

Moments later, she appeared once more.

"Yes, baby," Mrs. Virginia said.

Rolla gestured towards Drip.

Drip then peeled off twenty more $100 bills and handed them to the old lady, who accepted them gladly.

"In the name of Jesus, our Lord and Savior, thank you, baby," Mrs. Virginia said, embracing Drip and planting a kiss on his cheek bone.

"You're welcome, ma'am. Your grandson is a smart young man. He accepted the job I have awaiting him. This is part of his advance money," Drip explained, then handed Rolla $3,000 and a business card. "Hit me up tomorrow so we can go through the details of it all. A'ight. Around eleven in the A.M. will be a good time to catch me, bro."

Rolla accepted the offering and said he'd call.

The three then left. Drip played a classic chess move on Rolla. He was several moves ahead of him, a thinker in every sense of the word.

****

Two Weeks Later . . .
Rolla contacted Brazy to discuss a potential business deal with him, Tank, and Polo. They were also invited to a birthday party he was hosting, dubbed "Blood Boy Birthday Bash." Rolla, along with another associate posing as a Blood member (Animal), wanted them to celebrate together and urged them to attend, promising that they would be protected thoroughly and have a good time. Rolla made the drive to the Steel City to pick them up. He was able to convince them to leave their guns behind, adding that the Blood homies in Philly had plenty of fire-power to protect them and that they had nothing to fear. Besides, they didn't want to run the risk of getting pulled over, four niggaz deep in a car, by the state troopers, because they'd surely get booked, no doubt. They agreed to travel without guns.

While on the ride back from Pittsburgh, Rolla texted Drip to let him know they were on the way, unarmed.

Drip owned a house in South Philly he rarely used. It had a garage to it. The spot was situated in a bustling neighborhood where loud disturbances were common—a perfect location to muffle gunshots if needed.

Upon arriving at the house, Animal had music blaring and party lights flashing. Rolla parked the car in the garage. Animal lowered the door. Immediately, Body, Cold Heart, Hound Jr., and Monk emerged with AK-47 rifles and Mossberg pump-action shotguns, aiming at them. Animal approached Brazy's side of the car with his Glock .40 drawn as well. He ordered him out slowly. Brazy complied, stunned by the apparent set-up. He looked on at Rolla with his mouth wide and in a state of disbelief.

Brazy, tall at six-eight, was decked out in red and black Blood attire from head to toe, sporting tattoos and shoelaces fashioned into "Five Point Stars." He wore red Converse Chuck Taylors and an expensive black and red linen suit to match.

"You know what it is, slime nigga! Get your motherfuckin' hands up!" Animal ordered.

Wham!

Cold Heart struck Brazy from behind with his shotgun, causing him to collapse onto the concrete floor. Animal then zip-tied his hands and legs. Tank and Polo exited the car and willingly got down to the floor, where they were also tied up—at the wrist and ankles.

Drip then appeared. He wanted to have a few words with Brazy. Animal flipped him onto his back so to look up as Drip spoke to him.

"So we meet again, don't we! But this time, under different circumstances," Drip stated.

"Yeah! We do. But what's this shit all about? And what you got going on, Blood? How you flip the script of us like that, Rolla! Blood in, Blood out, nigga! Ain't no two ways about it!" Brazy barked at Rolla.

"Nigga, last I checked, Blood gang ain't putting no food on the table or no bread in my pocket, like my homie Drip is. And my Philly homies are my real brothers. Besides, nigga, I've known Drip and his squad long before the Blood gang anyway. And y'all niggaz from Pittsburgh anyway. Philly run PA! So you right. It ain't no two ways about it. It is what it is, dawg!" Rolla retorted.

"Y'all gag them niggaz and shut'em the fuck up!" Drip ordered. "Then load'em in the van. I gotta give them to some others as a special treat."

All of Drip's associates followed his instructions diligently. He then handed Rolla an additional thirty grand, promising to finalize the deal the next day. They exchanged daps, and Drip allowed Rolla to depart.

Before loading Brazy and the others into the mini-van, Drip had Body take all their phones, money, and jewelry. Drip destroyed the phones there on the spot, and split the money and jewelry among his crew.

A Few Hours Later...

Drip and the crew arrived at the farm he owned in Williamsport, parking inside a barn nestled in the far corner of the land. A foul odor permeated the barn, causing everyone but Drip to gag and nearly retch. Though he was accustomed to it, having been there several times before, Body and Animal struggled to endure the horrific stench.

"Damn, fam! What the fuck!" Hound Jr. exclaimed.

Drip grinned with delight.

'Y'all get these bitch-ass niggaz out the van and over to the slaughter pen. It's time for my special treat to be delivered. The delicate meal I've got for my boys," he said, then walked over to a wood chipper in the corner of the barn.

"Animal, give me a hand, bro," he requested.

The homie walked over to assist him.

Drip and everyone else had on black jogging-suits and dark colored Durango and Timberland boots. They positioned the chipper near Brazy and his cohorts, who squirmed and pleaded for mercy upon realizing what awaited them, more so as Drip walked over to the tool shed and returned with five wooden baseball bats.

"Nah, nigga! Don't beg for mercy from me now! You and that nigga right here you sent to kill me (he pointed at Tank) didn't have any. So guess what? Me and my people not gonna have any either!" Drip stated, distributing baseball bats to Monk, Hound Jr., and his two associates, Animal and Body, while keeping one for himself.

"Time to say bye-bye, niggaz! We're gonna have a 'Blood Birthday Massacre' to celebrate the death of you niggaz! Right here, right now! I'll see you in hell, motherfuckas!"

Drip spat, raising his bat high before delivering a devastating blow to Brazy's forehead, splitting it badly.

His blow upon Brazy was cue for everybody else to follow the lead and bludgeon the others in the same way, all head strikes. The three were now sprawled out at the feet of their killers. They were stripped out of their clothes and rendered naked.

"Now for the fun part," Drip said, igniting the wood chipper.

One by one, they loaded the bodies into the chipper, beginning with Brazy. The machine obliterated the flesh and bones of the victims, leaving behind a thick gooey clumpy mound of human flesh at the middle of the muddy pen.

Drip then hit the switch on a small electric box that was mounted on the wall of the barn. A trapdoor to a stall in the back was opened. A buzzer sounded. Immediately, in rushed a pack of huge, ferocious and vicious African wild hogs. There were about twenty of them, black and dark rust-colored, eager for their feast.

"What the fuck!" Cold Heart exclaimed at the sight of the wild beasts.

"Drip! What the fuck! You a wild dude, fam! A wild dude!" Hound Jr. said.

Drip glanced at both Cold Heart and his cousin, chuckling maniacally. He'd transformed into a different persona when his hands were stained with blood. His loyal associates—Body, Monk, and Animal—had witnessed this side of him before, but it was new to the others.

"My boys were hungry. I had to feed them. Haven't had the chance to do so in while," Drip said. "And I love watching them eat."

"Shit! Yeah! We see!" remarked Hound Jr.

"Talk about making bodies disappear! This a real efficient way to do it," Cold Heart remarked."

"Damn sure is. And I hope they have a big appetite, 'cause we're gonna keep 'em well-fed," Drip added, snickering as the hogs feasted on the macabre meal." His loyal crew stared in horror, unable to believe what they were witnessing. As always, Drip delivered for those who remained loyal to him. Even to his animals he maintained.

PART THREE

Chapter 21

February 2010
Three Months Later . . .

After Thanksgiving Day had passed, a series of significant dates loomed on the horizon: Black Friday, Christmas Day, Hanukkah, Kwanzaa, and New Year's Day. In the interim between these holidays, a multitude of events unfolded following the club shooting. Both Von and his mom had been indicted for the killing of Bernard, and received comprehensive discovery packages containing all the evidence the state intended to wield against them in trial. Despite this mounting evidence, Von staunchly chose to go to trial on both murder charges, adamantly rebuffing every plea offer presented by the District Attorney's office. The first trial, concerning the Kavon Lassiter killing, was set to begin in precisely one week. Subsequently, the joint trial involving Von and his mother was slated to begin four weeks after the conclusion of his first trial. Central to the prosecution's case were the testimonies of three eyewitnesses; Jeffery Toliver, Tobias Flowers, and his girlfriend, Ella. The urgent task at hand was to locate each of these witnesses, as Von possessed their identities and current addresses within his discovery package, rendering it an invaluable source.

Reflecting on the events of the day he eliminated Lassiter, Von recalled encountering Tobias speeding away in his Beamer immediately after the shooting. Contemplating

Tobias's subsequent betrayal, Von mused, *I never thought he'd turn rat though. Being the type of street nigga he claimed to be. I didn't see that coming. But here we are. And the nigga has his bitch in the car with him. They both gonna get it,* he concluded.

Driven by his resolve, Von placed a call to his homie Cold Heart, using the jail phone affixed to the wall.

"Yo, Vonnie! How you holding up, bro? You good?"

"Nah, not hardly," Von responded solemnly.

"What's going on, man? How can I help?" Cold Heart asked.

"Got my discovery. I know exactly who is supposed to be ratting now."

"Oh, really?"

"Hell yeah. I know where they live too."

"Who?"

"You remember the nigga, Tobias, don't you?"

"Talking about the dude from around the way who used to box?"

"Right. That was his spot I was aiming to let JT have the day that thing went down. Apparently, the nigga Tobias and his girl was somewhere around when dude got dome called. He stated to the police it was me. Him and that bitch of his. Now remembering, I do recall seeing his black Beamer leave the area right there in the moment."

"Yeah, I remember that nigga. Tobias Flowers, right?"

"Right. He used to box heavy with Yuself Mack, Nitty, and them other niggaz over at Shular's Gym out west. I remember you and one of their boys had a fight at Blue Horizon."

"I remember all them niggaz. I remember them really good. But say no more. I got you. I know what to do."

"Bet. And about that nigga, JT—I thought you got a hand on that nigga already?" Von asked.

"Nah. I wasn't able to. I gotta relocate him again."

"I got the nigga's new address. Here. Write it down. This his mom's spot. They moved from the old one," Von said.

Cold Heart documented all the information related to him. He vowed to Vonnie that by the time the trial was to begin, he'd have all the "dirty dishes in the kitchen sink" cleansed and out the way, so not to mess him up.

"Oh. I almost forgot, bro," Cold Heart interjected suddenly.

"What's that, Cold?"

"We found out who the nigga was that shot you," he revealed.

"Really?" Von's interest piqued.

"For sho. We found out who sent him, and what everything was all about."

"Talk to me. I need to hear this."

"They wasn't aiming to hit you. Drip was the target."

"What!"

"Yep. Him and some blood nigga had a beef. A nigga from Pittsburgh."

"What's the deal with 'em—The shooter and the one who sent him?" Von asked.

"It's over with for 'em. All the way over with. That's a story there I really gotta tell you about in due time. But your fam, Drip . . . That nigga gotta wicked side to him! A real dark wicked side, bro. You might not know the half of it," Cold Heart chuckled.

"Yeah, you definitely gotta tell me about it when I'm free. But look, I'mma let you go on about your night. I don't want to slow you down, bro. I'm on the clock, Cold. We can't let nobody show up to give their 'Easter Speech' on me. Okay?"

"Relax, bro. You know I got you. Just take care up in there and be easy, my nigga," Cold Heart stated.

"That's what's up. I know you on top of shit," Von responded before a thought struck him. "Aye, also, 'bout, our homie Lonnie. You know he's up in here with me too, right?" Von revealed.

"Word! Fuck he do? Ain't heard nothing about that," Cold Heart responded.

"It ain't too much. He and his girl got into a fight. He got on her ass, and she called the cops."

"When this happen?"

"About a week ago."

"Oh, okay. It ain't too serious. That's probably why Kareem never mentioned it to me"

"How is everybody else in the crew doing? Shay and Tangee been holding shit down since Cori been booked?" Von asked.

"Shay not around no more, bro," Cold Heart revealed.

"Huh! What happened?"

"We'll speak on that some other time, bro. But she not around no more at all," he said sombrely.

"Damn. That's crazy."

"Hey, life has to go on. But Tangee locked in with Monk still. So you know she's good. We still got the upstate spot doing numbers, and all the other blocks here in the city. And your baby by Cori is doing well too, bro. I made it my business to go by to see Shay's mom. You know she's the one taking care of Cori's kids."

"You bless them, right?"

"You know I did, bro. I gave the mom thirty thousand. I'mma keep some bread in her hand. It's only right that I do."

"No doubt. You gotta do your duty and mine too, until I'm free again."

"That's what real homies are for, bro. But look, I'mma be sure those two fucks are a no show."

"That's a bet. Be easy," Von lastly said.

"You too, bro."

The call ended.

Cold Heart pondered meticulously, strategizing on how to permanently silence the three principal witnesses.

****

Not long after Chloe gave birth to the son she and Von shared, Rosa followed suit. Welcoming a baby girl into the world, she named her Talandra Marie Savage. Talandra arrived on November 24th, just three days after Von's birthday. Chloe had a son, whom she named after Von.

Chloe and Rosa had both returned to work at their regular jobs. The two had also put money together and started a small business, establishing a janitorial service. On weekends and during the week, they diligently attended to their business duties, sometimes enlisting the help of a couple of female cousins to fulfill contracts. The Dominquez Cleaning Services soon gained momentum, operating at full capacity.

Lily dedicated herself to spending ample time with her three grandkids, alongside facing the impending courtroom showdown concerning the charges Von was out on bail for.

True to his word, Hound Jr. secured a building for the boutique Lily had always dreamed of. It was located on South Street. Lily, along with her two close friends—Stella Jamison and Tommie Slaughter—managed the shop.

With the dawn of a new era came both prosperity and anxiety. Optimism abounded, yet worries about the uncertainties of the future lingered.

Hound Jr., driven by a new-found ambition, aggressively pursued success in the realms of hustling and business. Shedding the rust accumulated during his absence from the game, he made strategic moves from the get-go. The profits from his burgeoning business were reinvested into legitimate ventures, primarily targeting services deemed essential in black communities: Laundromats, dry cleaners, vehicle detailing centers, and vending machine set-ups. Additionally, he allocated a significant portion of his earnings to Drip, facilitating investments in high-end property development projects. Drip hinted at having a stake in the future renovation of the Gallery Mall, slated to transform it into Philadelphia's Fashion District.

However, amidst his rise, Hound Jr. harbored resentment towards the lead homicide detective handling his son's case. Desiring a personal meeting with William (Bill) Hilliard, Hound Jr. sought to discern the detective's motives and potential political ambitions, suspecting his son was being exploited for personal gain.

Discussing his intentions with Drip over lunch at Carmine's Italian restaurant, Hound Jr. aimed to leverage Drip's connections to arrange a meeting with Bill. Drip wanted to invest money with Hound Jr. to boost the purchasing power of the new product he firmly believed would shape the future of his business endeavors. This presented him with the perfect opportunity to do just that.

The Savage boys had arrived in style, clad in high-end designer attire, their Range Rover trucks gleaming out front the eatery.

Drip and Hound Jr. were seated at a table with Carmine. While Drip and Carmine were somewhat familiar with each other due to their families' long history of acquaintanceship, they hadn't formed a personal connection like the one between Hound Jr. and Carmine.

"Italian clothing worn by you two . . . meets Italian food and Italian gangsters. What a wonderful culmination," Carmine remarked. "Nice to meet you two on this lovely day, the first of March."

They all shook hands.

"Nice to meet you again too, Carmine. This here is my people I was telling you about—Damien," said Hound Jr.

Carmine and Drip exchanged strong eye contact, recognizing the alpha-male energy and dominant mindset each possessed.

"Pleasure to meet you, Damien," said Carmine.

"Likewise. I understand that our families have extensive ties to one another. The Savages and Marconis have rich history."

"Indeed, we do, don't we."

"My dad and his granddad Mickey, are first cousins," Hound Jr. said to Carmine.

"Oh! Mickey his grandfather, huh?" Carmine said as he lit up at the mention of Mickey's name. He became more comfortable with Drip at that point.

Drip pulled out his phone and showed Carmine a few photos from his gallery. One stood out the most, featuring his grandpa, Hound Jr.'s dad, their cousin Johnny Mack, Carmine's grandpa Angelo, Angelo's brother Pete, and Carmine's pop Raphael, together in them. Their faces were clearly visible.

"So, you'll know I'm authentic," Drip remarked, a welcoming smile on his face.

Carmine returned the smile. "I see. The three of us are off to a damn good start, aren't we?"

"Indeed, we are," chimed in Hound Jr.

"Let's get down to business, shall we?" Carmine urged.

The trio then dove into the business discussion they were there for. Promises were made and secured with the new Meth supply. Drip intended to let Hound Jr. continue handling that particular department as he already had it under control. Besides, Hound Jr. had his sights set on owning a gentlemen's club that would welcome only a mature clientele.

Drip got a text from one his top people, Pervis, the police detective brother of Body. Drip had contacted him the night before, wanting him to meet with him and his cousin so the two could get more acquainted with each other. Since Pervis was off that day and had some free time, Drip texted him the address of the restaurant they were at. He wasn't too far away, having been in and around the city for the past two hours. His home was in West Chester, Pennsylvania, not too distant from Philly.

Carmine excused himself from the group, feeling good about the connection he and Drip had made, thanks in large part to Hound Jr.

****

Thirty Minutes Later . . .

Pervis arrived at the eatery, where he, Drip, and Hound Jr., exchanged handshakes and embraces. Pervis felt comfortable enough to let his street demeanor shine in Drip's presence, as they had known each other for many years, dating back to Drip and Body's days in middle school and varsity.

"What's good with you, bro? How is your day going so far?" Drip greeted.

"Everything well, bro. I can't complain. What about you two?" Pervis responded in his signature deep voice, reminiscent of the legendary soul music singer, Issac Hayes, with his shaved head, full dark beard, and slightly plump nose.

"Yeah. We good. This is my people here again. Y'all briefly met before. Cornelius is his name, if you may remember," Drip stated.

"How are you, Pervis?" Hound Jr. asked.

"Prosperous."

"Likewise."

Drip spoke up again. "You had a chance to get that info for me? About the Bill Hilliard dude I asked you about?"

"No doubt. I know a lot about him, on top of what you wanna know," Pervis explained. "He's a hard-liner. Very career-oriented. Chained to the force. A former military guy. Went from there to being at the department. Don't know much else to do for himself in life but law enforcement. He's a serious cop."

"You think he'll be open to a sit-down for a conversation? Reason being, my son is now booked on two counts of murder up in the county, as you may know. He and his mom have an upcoming court date on one of them. I wanna talk with him. Why he's so hell-bent on trying to put my boy away? What's his angle?" Hound Jr. laid out his intentions.

"The best thing I can tell you on that is to simply pull up on him and impose the type of conversation you're looking to have. He loves to do lunch at the Starbucks one block down from the department, from twelve to one any day through the work week. He and his Puerto Rican sidekick, Valente Canelo," Pervis stated.

"Canelo!" Hound Jr. exclaimed. "Why does that family name sound familiar to me?"

"Beats me, fam," remarked, Drip.

"It'll come to me before long, I'm sure."

"Okay, look. More than likely, we're gonna need more information on both Bill and Canelo," Drip said.

"Not a problem. And look, don't forget, we got an important meeting with the 'WM' on the third. He wants everybody from the second degree on up to be present," Pervis reminded.

"Seven sharp, right?" Drip said.

"No doubt. You already know. The three of us are lined up under the same enlightener, you feel me," Pervis stated.

"WM? Enlightener? What is that all about?" Hound Jr. asked.

"Oh, that's something else there, fam. I'mma guide you to that point sometime soon. Be patient. That's a whole different world there. Illuminati three-sixty. That's the life we live," explained Drip.

"Masonic talk, I see," Hound Jr remarked with a smile

"For sho', fam. We on it."

Pervis, his brother Body, and their friend Drip were all initiated into the Prince Hall Masonic order. Pervis was the

Master Mason of the 3rd degree, while Body and Drip were at the 2nd degrees (companions of the Master Mason). He had the responsibility of guiding the younger two in that regard and was sure to protect them in all their endeavors. The Worshipful Master, a former Federal Judge of the Philadelphia Grand Lodge, ordered that everyone meet on the 3rd of each month, the 7th, and the 9th. The upcoming event they needed to be present for was the advancement in rank ceremony for a few within the circle.

Drip then retrieved a brown paper bag from his coat pocket and handed it to Pervis. It was thick and filled with cash—two hundred and fifty $100 bills.

"Here you go, bro. Five thousand goes to the lodge, and the remaining twenty you keep. You're gonna be able to make that happen, right?"

"No doubt, I will. You don't have to worry about dude saying nothing on your people. He'll be dealt with by the time they go to pick him up to be placed into protective custody. No face, no case," Pervis responded.

Drip chuckled at the phrase Pervis used. "I ain't heard you say that in a minute. That street shit still runs through your blood, don't it?"

"That street shit ain't never left my blood, playboy. I just learned how to handle it better. I have to, because of the job I have and the people I encounter daily," Pervis said, putting. the paper bag away.

The three then stood up and exited together. With the hope that the work Drip hired him to do would be completed soon, Pervis felt the need to reassure Drip that everything would be taken care of. He recognized a concerned look in his young friend's eyes.

"I got it handled, Drip. You know I do."

"I know you do, bro. I just gotta be sure my family good."

Pervis then observed the both of them once more before they went their separate ways for the day. He'd parked around the block from the restaurant.

Drip was driving alone that day. He gave his cousin a hug, then got into his truck and pulled away. There was another meeting he had to attend—one with a distributor of his. A white guy with whom he had serious business. The two had a working relationship. His name was Harley Ferguson, and he owned an Irish Pub called "Flannigans," located in Northeast Philly.

Hound Jr. made his way to see Daniella after her classes at the college had ended for the day. They hadn't seen one another physically in a few days. She had been extra busy studying and preparing for exams prior to the upcoming spring break. They both were eager to fuck. She loved the way her OG boyfriend took command of things without pestering her like older men typically would with young females. And he cherished everything about her. She kept him young and vigorous. She was every alpha-male's fantasy.

However, he was still busy busting his brain trying to remember where he recalled that name Canelo from. It was now a priority of his to know. He felt duty-bound to do so.

Chapter 22

Two Weeks Later . . .

Cold Heart was deadly serious about tracking down JT and putting him away for good. The address provided by Von, a crucial lead in his investigation, turned out to be a dead end. In a panic, JT relocated himself and his mother across the bridge to Cherry Hill, New Jersey. Both federal agents and the Philadelphia homicide division were content with this move, as it meant less effort on their part to protect him, so long as he stayed out of their way. However, JT was far from safe yet.

Despite his precarious situation, JT was careless, constantly active on Facebook and frequently engaging with strangers on Messenger. Unbeknownst to him, he left his location signal on, allowing anyone he communicated with to easily track him down. Furthermore, the new address he acquired was discovered by a hired hitman who now patiently stalked him, awaiting the perfect opportunity to strike.

One fateful night, the hitman sat in a getaway car near a train stop in Cherry Hill, knowing JT would soon return from Philadelphia after a long day of shopping at the Gallery Mall. The hitman ingeniously set a trap, posing as a woman on Messenger to lure JT into a false sense of security.

As JT stepped off the train and descended the platform with his shopping bags, completely unaware of the danger lurking nearby, the hitman sprang into action. With calculated precision, he maneuvered the car towards JT, who was absorbed in conversation on his phone. JT never had the chance to turn around before the hitman opened fire. The sound of gunfire echoed through the quiet streets as Pervis— the hitman—executed his plan flawlessly. He knew that eliminating JT, who was likely to testify against Von, was crucial. Drip, his employer, couldn't afford to let JT become an available witness. Not under any circumstances.

****

One Day Before Von's Trial Begins . . .

With one target eliminated and two others to go, Von could finally exhale, albeit momentarily. His trial loomed less than 24 hours away, and he needed assurance that the snitch-ass nigga Tobias and that bitch of his Ella, were permanently silenced, ensuring they wouldn't testify against him. Assistant District Attorney Brian Shapiro, known for his steely resolve and calculated demeanor, was primed and poised to prosecute Von to the fullest extent of the law. Despite losing one potential witness, Shapiro remained undeterred, confident in his ability to secure a conviction with the remaining testimony.

The address given to Cold Heart to locate Tobias and Ella proved accurate. They maintained a transient lifestyle, alternating between Tobias's aunt's residence in North Philly and various hotels. Cold Heart sought insight from the street-savvy twins, Khaddafi and Khalil, regarding Tobias's affiliations and potential whereabouts. Satisfied with their intel, Cold Heart enlisted their aid in orchestrating the hits.

Surprisingly, Tobias and Ella proved more of accessible targets than anticipated. Positioned strategically in the darkness of the night, Cold Heart and his team (prominent among whom were Fat Steve and Heem) lay in wait near Tobias's aunt's house. The four hitters waited in the alley behind. As the couple emerged, preparing to depart in Tobias's BMW, Cold Heart signaled the start of the assault.

Cold Heart called Heem.

"Yo!" Heem answered.

"Go!" Cold Heart replied, giving the order to kill.

The four shooters ran from the back of the house. They were all clad in black with ski-masks covering their faces.

Tobias and the girlfriend only had enough time to take a seat in the car and him put the key in the ignition before the shooters turned the corner of the house facing them and began blasting.

Boom—Boom—Boom!

Pop—Pop—Pop!

Pow—Pow—Pow!

Boc—Boc—Boc!

Gun fire sprayed from four different high caliber pistols. With precision, the shooters unleashed a barrage of gunfire, striking Tobias and Ella multiple times before fleeing the scene.

Everyone then ran off. Amidst the chaos, no witnesses remained to recount the deadly encounter, sparing any further casualties. Tobias and Ella would be conspicuously absent from court proceedings, ensuring Von's protection under the veil of his Savage family empire. The dominance of Von's criminal syndicate left no room for doubt. Justice, in this realm, was unequivocally served.

Chapter 23

The first trial for Von was set to begin on this particular day. It was the second Monday of March 2010. Assistant District Attorney Brian Shapiro, representing the State of Pennsylvania, had meticulously prepared to present the prosecution's case. On the defense side, Von's legal team was ready with an alibi defense, poised to demonstrate his complete innocence on all charges. Von felt confident that with everything aligned in his favor, the outcome would be favorable.

The jury pool awaited selection in the spectator section, and all witnesses gathered in separate rooms, ready to testify.

Von's family and his significant others were present, including his parents, grandparents, friends, and siblings. Introductions were made among those unfamiliar with each other, though tension simmered beneath the surface, particularly evident in exchanges between Monyetta aad Kidada with Chloe and Rosa.

"I'm sorry, how long have you been involved with Trevon again?" Chloe asked Monyetta in a sarcastic tone. "I didn't catch that part."

"She's been involved just as long as you have, honey," Kidada chimed in to speak for the soft-spoken, shy Monyetta.

"She can't speak for herself?" Rosa now put her two cents in it.

"She doesn't have to when I'm doing it for her, now does she! And who gave you permission to speak!" Kidada fired back. "Who are you to my brother anyway? That's what I'd like to know?"

"Well, if you must know," Chloe began, "we're both mothers to Vonnie's kids. That's who *we* are to *your* brother!".

The atmosphere grew strained as passive-aggressive remarks flew, prompting Lily to intervene and urge unity for Von's sake. "Ladies, ladies, ladies!" said Lily to hush them up. "Could y'all please calm down, be cordial, and let's stand together for my son? We've got more important *ish* to deal with than an unpleasant exchange of attitudes. Alright?"

"I'm telling you. Damn!" Hound Jr. uttered. Despite attempts to diffuse the situation, tensions lingered, observed disapprovingly by others in attendance.

Hound Sr. and Henrietta simply shook their heads in disbelief at the way the girls behaved.

"And it's nice to finally meet you, Monyetta. When this is over, and my boy freed, us ladies gonna all go out and have a conversation to talk about everything. It's a special reason why we're all here together. My Vonnie is the reason. So y'all take a chill pill, and think over that, won't you!" Lily said.

Kidada took Lily's words literally. Acting on impulse, the rebellious young woman reached into her Fendi purse, grabbed a Percocet from the plastic bag, and swallowed it with a gulp of her bottled water. She then returned to her seat on the bench, stating, "I'll talk with you two later!"

Shortly thereafter, Von, accompanied by his attorney Levi Jacobson, entered the courtroom, impeccably dressed in a Salvatore Ferragamo suit. Despite the charged atmosphere, Von maintained a composed demeanor, acknowledging the presence of his companions with a smile. However, his gaze shifted with concern upon noticing the proximity of his three girlfriends and sisters, separated only by Kidada. Shaking his head, he smiled once more to diffuse the tension.

"I have very good news for you, Trevon," the lawyer Levi said to him.

"And what's that?"

"Don't know if you were aware or not through the news. But all three key witnesses the state was intending to use, will not be available. Apparently they were murdered. Jeffrey Toliver, the one who claimed to have a friendship with you—"

"I've never heard of him. Don't know anything about dude," Von cut in to say.

"Well, regardless of his intentions toward you, he's no longer a concern," Jacobson stated.

"Is that right. What happened?" Von inquired.

"He was slain in a drive-by shooting not long ago in New Jersey."

"Damn! He'd pissed somebody off, didn't he?"

"You bet your ass, he did."

"And what happened to the other two?" Von asked.

"Oh! Flowers and the girlfriend. Somebody must have had it out bad for those two as well."

"Why do you say that?"

Jacobson locked eyes with Von, attempting to gauge whether he was genuinely unaware or simply feigning ignorance.

Jacobson continued. "A heavy downpour of lead rained upon Flowers and his girl just last night. Not even twelve hours ago."

Von took a look at the lawyer's watch out of the corner of his eye. It read 9:22 A.M. He and the defense attorney then leaned back into their seats. Court was nearly in session.

Von turned his head slightly to lock eyes with Cold Heart. They winked at each other. He then leaned in to have another word with his lawyer.

"By those three witnesses not being available, what's that supposed to mean, Mister Jacobson?"

"It means, more than likely, they don't have nearly enough to prove guilt or anything. And I imagine, the ADA Shapiro—"

"A real dickhead, from what I've heard!" Von interjected.

"He could be a hard-on at times. That's his job as a prosecutor. He's essentially a surrogate for Andrew Clavenski. But don't take it personally. He only acts on orders from his superiors or suggestions from his close detective buddy, Bill Hilliard."

"You talking 'bout that stubby black Sambo-looking ass nigga with the Rican partner, right?"

Jacobson, taken aback by the sarcastic insult Von made, paused to consider his response. He was Jewish and had never encountered such overt racism from a client before.

"If you're referring to the police detective named Willliam 'Bill' Hilliard, then yes, that be the guy," Jacobson said.

"I'm familiar with who you're talking 'bout. They interviewed me on a few occasions. I definitely didn't like how it went."

"But, as I was saying, being that these three witnesses won't be available, Shapiro may move to try and have the trial continued."

"Oh no! That ain't going down like that. I'm ready to get this shit over and done with."

"And I intend to strongly object to any attempts to delay the trial."

"No matter what, Mister Jacobson, don't allow that to happen," Von pleaded with his lawyer. "No continuances."

"It won't. The court calendar is too loaded anyway, and both sides have announced that we're ready."

"No doubt," Von replied.

"All rise!" the bailiff exclaimed. "The honorable Judge Helen Lockhart presides."

In walked the African-American, well cultivated, and slim female interpreter of the law. Everyone rose to their feet.

"You may be seated," Lockhart said as she settled firmly into the plush leather chair available for her. She then opened the file and proceeded to recite the case at hand.

"This is the case of The State of Pennsylvania commonwealth versus Trevon Aaron Dietrich-Savage, the defendant in the case. Is the defendant present?"

"Present, your honor," Jacobson stood and stated. "Levi Jacobson represents the defense."

"And who's present on behalf of the State?"

"I am, judge. ADA Brian Shapiro," the prosecutor stood to his feet and made the court aware.

"Very well."

Judge Lockhart then looked sternly at the defendant, at Levi Jacobson, and then at Shapiro. Her eyes went back and forth, from one attorney they went to the next, shaking her head in the process. Of the many times Jacobson had appeared before her with a client, never before had she known the well-polished, aristocratic, and affluent lawyer, to represent someone from the extreme lower end of society, someone such as Von. Truth be told, Von was the most low-profile, low-class person he'd ever taken on, and both Shapiro and Jacobson's two assistants knew it.

She eyed Von one more time then proceeded. Her thoughts and all she knew about the case at hand ran rampant. "Interesting client you have there, Mister Jacobson," Judge Lockhart remarked.

"Yeah!" blurted Shapiro to make mockery of the defense lawyer. He was struggling to control himself.

To those who knew, the judge's comment was obvious to what she referred.

"Yes, judge. That he is. A very smart young man, who has a bright and promising future ahead of him. Once we're able to move forward past this. And I'm sure we shall."

155

"Not hardly. It won't be that easy," Shapiro remarked.

"Gentlemen! We haven't even seated a jury and you two are slinging mud already," said the judge. "We're not going to have this. Not at all."

"Apologies, Your Honor," Jacobson said first.

"Likewise, judge," Shapiro added.

"Very well. Now, before we proceed with jury selection, Voir Dire, and opening statements, is there anything that needs to be brought to the attention of the court? We'll start with the State—you, Mister Shapiro?"

"Yes, Your Honor, throughout the past week, the state has received terrible news regarding the three crucial eye-witnesses whom were set to testify."

"And that is?"

"Tragically, the three witnesses I make mention of are no longer with us. I intend to make the court wholly aware of the details surrounding the sudden unavailability of the witnesses in question at the fit opportunity, Your Honor."

"This sounds to me like you have a request in the pipeline, Mister Shapiro. Do you?"

"Yes, judge. That's correct."

"I'm listening."

"Your Honor, the state would like to ask the court to order a continuance of the trial. So that a rearrangement of the witness list be made and the state be afforded the proper opportunity to present its case," Shapiro said.

"Objection, Your Honor," Jacobson stood to his feet and stated. "My client has been unfairly arrested and taken down on the charges for several months now, and is prepared to literally prove his innocence beginning today, and put this ordeal behind him as soon as possible. We ask that no continuance be granted and that a jury be assembled to hear the case. Thank you."

"Mister Shapiro, do you want to respond to that?" Judge Lockhart asked.

"Absolutely, Your Honor. . . ."

The argument between the two attorneys went on and on. The argument lasted roughly a half hour before Judge Lockhart had heard more than she could take on one particular issue.

"The court will now take a thirty-minute break to consider the request put before me, and will return with a ruling. Additionally, both counsels are to report to my chambers to discuss the details surrounding the witnesses' unavailability. I will not compromise either the defendant's rights or the state's case. Court is adjourned." With a decisive gavel slam, Judge Lockhart exited for her chambers.

The bailiff escorted Von out a side door while the courtroom emptied. Jacobson and Shapiro were summoned to meet Judge Lockhart in private.

"Mister Shapiro," she began, "you may now elaborate on your request for a continuance."

"Sure, judge. If I may."

Shapiro and Jacobson presented their arguments, each attempting to sway the judge in their favor. Judge Lockhart listened intently for twenty minutes before delivering her verdict.

Shapiro's request for a two-month continuance was met with firm opposition. Judge Lockhart, burdened with heavy case-loads and a ready defense, was unimpressed by his tactic. She recognized Shapiro's ploy—to utilize the police investigation into the murders of three witnesses and potentially link them to Von. As a seasoned prosecutor, Shapiro understood the importance of evidence and its impact on his case.

"Mister Shapiro," Judge Lockhart stated firmly, "a two-month continuance is absolutely out of the question. However, acknowledging the unfortunate deaths of these potential witnesses who were crucial to the state's case, I propose a compromise. A three-day continuance will be granted. We will reconvene on Thursday for jury selection and opening statements can commence on Friday."

"But Your Honor—"

Jacobson tried to interject, but Judge Lockhart silenced him with a raised palm.

"Save it, Mister Jacobson. It's not necessary. My decision is made."

Judge Lockhart then freed them of her chambers to return to the courtroom.

The judge reconvened the court, to inform everyone of the ruling. Von was brought back in, followed by the spectators.

"What's the hold-up, counselor?" Von inquired of Jacobson.

Jacobson explained, "I fought for a same-day trial, but the judge won't budge. Three days is better than three months, though. Don't worry, this won't hurt your case—as long as they don't find anything new."

Von smirked. "From the looks of it, they ain't got much to begin with."

"Exactly!"

The court day wrapped up. Von was returned to the county jail. Everyone else dispersed, anticipating their return in three days.

Chapter 24

Two Days Later . . .

Hound Jr. was ready to act on Pervis's suggestion: If he wanted a word with Detective Bill Hilliard, all he had to do was approach him between noon and one any week day at the Starbucks near the police station. Lily had pointed Bill out when they left the courthouse, so Hound Jr. now knew what he looked like.

Hound Jr. found himself out and about in the city, alone for the afternoon. As lunchtime approached, a craving for fresh chocolate chip cookies and a large cappuccino hit him. What better place in America, he thought, than a Starbucks to fulfill this desire?

Parking in front, he entered the establishment and scanned the room. A mix of people filled the space—cops, office workers, students, and everyday citizens. In the back corner, pecking at his Blackberry, sat the one person he was looking for: Bill Hilliard.

Hound Jr. placed his order, received it, and made his way to the back where Bill and his partner, Valco, sat. He didn't bother asking permission before taking a seat.

"Good afternoon, gentlemen," he greeted them, taking a bite of a cookie as he sat down.

Both Bill and Valco stared at him, shocked by his actions

"You're at the wrong table, I believe," Bill said, then jolted in recognition. He remembered Hound Jr. from the hospital the night Von, Lily, and Ayonna were shot.

"Nah, I'm positive I'm at the right one. You're Bill Hilliard, correct? The same guy I had a brief encounter with the night my son was injured, then later wrongfully arrested. His trial began this week."

"I don't readily recall who you are. Hopefully you have some helpful information for us. If not, what do you want?"

"What do I want, you ask? For starters, I want to know, what's the beef you seem to have with my boy? You appear to have it out for him. In the worse way. Why?"

"Ahhh! I see where we're going with this. You feel as though I have some vendetta with the killer Savage boy."

"My boy ain't no goddamn killer!" Hound Jr. fired back. "As we'll surely prove when the trial resumes."

"The evidence says otherwise," Bill countered. "But what explanation do I owe you?"

"An explanation is not what I'm looking for," Hound Jr. remarked, a hint of aggression in his voice. "But a reason behind your madness would suffice."

Bill and Valco looked at him sternly, trying to gauge his energy. Hound Jr. had both hands on the table and visible to them, posing no physical threat. He simply seemed to want a man-to-man conversation.

"Sir, let me help you understand a thing or two about the troubles your boy has with the law."

"Please do. That's why I'm here. To engage you personally on the subject."

Hound Jr.'s visit now raised more questions than answers. Bill and Valco wondered if he may have had inside connections, considering he'd found Bill at the cafe during his specific lunch time hour.

"Who are we speaking with?" Valco finally asked, already half knowing the truth.

"I'm Cornelius Savage Junior. A man who's making great progress in the world."

"And what *exactly* do you do?" Bill sarcastically asked. "We missed that part."

Hound Jr. met Bill's gaze with a smile and a slight shake of his head, refusing to answer the jab.

"I see you're every bit of the character you were made out to be, my guy," Hound Jr. stated directly to Bill, likely referencing Pervis's words.

"Oh, I am!" Bill replied. "Thank you for noticing. Now back to your son. We have a plethora of evidence and material we're gonna paste him with in this trial and in the next one to follow. The momma included. For aiding and abetting. And the charges we've filed? They'll stick, no doubt. Your son is a menace, Cornelius. We have proof of his involvement in a multitude of ways regarding the ongoing investigations we're conducting," he stated emphatically.

"I disagree," Hound Jr. countered. "Once Trevon is cleared of these bogus charges, you'll back down and find a safer game to play in. We don't retreat. Not ever." His voice was laced with steely resolve.

Bill's eyes narrowed. "Is that a threat, sir?"

Hound Jr. scoffed. "No threat intended. Just a fact. Like your cholesterol and blood sugar levels. If that scares you, then maybe you should take my words seriously." He took a leisurely sip of his drink and munched on a cookie, his gaze fixed on Bill.

Bill glared back, a dark fire simmering in his eyes. The cheap shot hadn't gone unnoticed.

Bill's face burned with anger. Years of taunts about his weight had carved a deep insecurity upon him, and Hound Jr.'s words were a fresh wound, especially considering the health scares he had experienced. Here was a man hurling verbal shots at him for simply doing his job as a police veteran. Bill retaliated by firing back.

"Let me tell you something, you despicable scum bag, worthless criminal, and aging thug!" he bellowed, rising from his seat.

Valco extended his arm to restrain Bill. Bill sat back down, leaning in to continue his retort at Hound Jr.

"I'mma make it my absolute priority to ensure that your delinquent son ends up at the very bottom of a prison cell, do you hear me? His ass is gonna get life twice over for both those murders he committed! So be sure to save enough money to buy commissary and care packages, because that little nigga boy of yours will be in it for the long haul. And my ADA buddy who is prosecuting him will be made aware of this visit, and my strongest desire to bury your son's black ass! I promise you that! My promise to you. My promise to you, mister!" Bill spat, a muscle ticking in his jaw as he finally got to his feet so he and Valco could leave.

Valco stood as well.

Hound Jr. met Bill's gaze with an icy chill. "Don't be surprised if a monkey-wrench gets thrown in your machine . . . *Billy Holiday Hilliard!* My boy is gonna walk! I promise you on that! Bank on it! We ain't done here, detective." Hound Jr said to Bill.

Bill didn't even dignify Hound Jr.'s last remark with a response. He simply continued to walk towards the exit of the building. The tension between him and Hound Jr. hung heavy in the air, a silent promise of a fight to come.

"Motherfuckin' Uncle Tom, no good, shade tree nigga!" Hound Jr. said to himself in a slightly louder tone.

He'd waged war with a highly respected police detective, and had no plans to back down. His son was his top priority, and he was all in on helping him out.

Chapter 25

At The County Jail . . .

Von felt more determined than ever to go to trial. This was a shot at freedom. With three key witnesses silenced, an acquittal for the Kavon Lassiter case seemed certain. A win here would make the state wary of pursuing charges for Bernard's death. He'd deal with that hurdle later. One step at a time.

Throughout his incarceration, Von and one of his closest homies, Lonnie, had been diligently building their network by connecting with dudes inside who could be of use once freed. Soon, they'd have the muscle they needed to solidify their power. They were confident their day of liberation was on the horizon. Von and Lonnie began discussing the start of Von's trial, which was less than twelve hours away.

"Lonnie," Von said, his voice laced with steely resolve, "Tobias and that bitch of his are no longer a threat. They won't testify. My people took care of them. Sent those fucks to rat heaven! And they're now in a better place."

Lonnie chuckled. "Damn, Vonnie! That's what's up. And what about that weak link we had on the team, JT? What's his status?"

Von's eyes narrowed. "Dealt with him too! He *won't* have the chance to betray us anymore."

"Good! He had it coming anyway. No one disrespects the BMB. It's a new generation, but the tradition holds."

"Motherfuckin' right," Von agreed. They shared a fist bump, a silent vow to uphold their ruthless code.

Chapter 26

The Next Morning . . .

The courtroom buzzed with anticipation. Von's lawyer, Levi Jacobson, prepared for a win, eager to add another "Not Guilty" verdict to his belt. Everyone from Monday's session returned, the intervening days feeling like a mere blip.

The court convened, a diverse jury was eventually sworn in. Jacobson skillfully used pre-emptive strikes to secure a favorable panel. Four hours later, twelve jurors and two alternates sat in the box, a mix of races and ages.

The prosecution's opening arguments consumed the first day. It was a flurry of dramatic pronouncements, painting an unsubstantiated picture of Von as a thug. They lacked concrete evidence . . . No motive . . . No witnesses placing him at the scene . . . Nothing. Von's alibi was iron-clad: he'd been at his grandmother's at the time the incident had occurred, a fact Mrs. Edna herself would attest to on the stand. Her testimony would be aimed at the older jurors, and most likely will hold more weight than the prosecutor's flimsy theory.

Day two saw the defense take the stage. Jacobson's opening arguments were concise. He saw no need to elaborate on non-existent points. "Let them keep digging their own hole," he explained to Von, a confident smile playing on his lips.

Von smiled at him in return.

The state then called their first witnesses, a parade of police officers culminating in the renowned homicide detective, William (Bill) Hilliard. Levi Jacobson secured a crucial victory prior to—a judge's order to "bifurcate" the case. This meant Bill couldn't breathe a word about Von's other murder investigation and potential trial to come. Any violation would result in a mistrial, a costly setback for the prosecution.

Shapiro and Jacobson ended examination of Bill, and the court adjourned for the weekend. Once Monday resumed, Valente Canelo would be taking the stand. Relief washed over the jury to be granted a break, although the trial had just gotten going. Excitement buzzed among spectators at the end day's results for the defense. Things were looking fairly good. Von was transported back to the county jail, buoyed by the apparent weakness of the case. "Weaker than baby pee," Jacobson had assured him, regarding the case.

****

Three Days Later . . .

The trial resumed, and all the previous attendees were present once again, with Valco on the stand. Shapiro's questioning mirrored his strategy with Bill, eliciting the same limited information. Jacobson's cross-examination was a breeze, emphasizing the state's inability to place Von at the scene of the execution style slaying.

"No further questions for the witness, Your Honor," Jacobson finally said.

"Very well. You may step down, Mister Canelo," Judge Lockhart stated. "Next witness, Mister Shapiro."

The medical examiner, who conducted the autopsy on Kavon Lassiter's body, was called to testify. He would be the last official to be examined. After him, it was supposed to have been the three eye witnesses. However, that was no longer the case.

The medical examiner's testimony confirmed the gunshot wound to the head, but Shapiro's attempt to portray the shooter as a cold-blooded killer—Vonnie, that is—backfired. The lack of details about the suspect's vehicle, a Dodge Magnum, became a point of contention. They'd messed up so bad, they had even forgotten to specify the *color* of the vehicle that was supposedly involved. Jacobson capitalized on the mistake.

"If we only knew how many Dodge Magnum auto mobiles exist in the Tri-State area, perhaps we could have an idea of who owns them," Jacobson quipped, drawing laughter from the jury and exposing the state's oversight.

The medical examiner was visibly relaxed after his testimony.

"No further witnesses by the state, Your Honor," Shapiro announced.

Shapiro's announcement of a closed case regarding witnesses seemed to surprise everyone. The jury, now keenly aware of the missing eyewitnesses and lack of concrete evidence, watched intensely, as Judge Lockhart adjourned court for the day. The state's case, built solely on police testimony, appeared flimsy in totality. Von, seemingly, was being framed. The defense awaited the chance to call their own witnesses as the trial entered its fourth day. Jacobson's strategy was working. Working very smoothly. Like a well-oiled machine.

****

One Day Later . . .

Everyone was present in court and ready for the continuation of the trial. Order was called and the session began.

"Mister Jacobson, is the defense ready to call its first witness?" Judge Lockhart asked.

"Yes, Your Honor. We are."

"Very well. Please proceed."

"Absolutely. The defense would like to call Miss Edna Dietrich to the stand, please, the grandmother of the defendant," Jacobson stated.

Mrs. Edna was then escorted from the witness room and took her place at the stand. Lily had dressed her mother in a stylish pink pants suit with appropriate accessories. Mrs. Edna, a late sixty-something biracial former beauty queen (her mother was a white, blue-eyed German and her father was an African-American male), had a pleasant smile and a graceful presence. Her shoulder-length hair was pinned near her ears, revealing her diamond-studded earrings. As always, Mrs. Edna's flawless skin and modest facial expressions were noticeable.

Once seated, she was sworn in and Jacobson began with his first set of questions. Mrs. Edna simply stated what she knew to be true—that her grandson was there with her on the day in question, having just returned home from school. It was absolutely impossible for him to have been both at school and involved in a shooting in a faraway location.

Mrs. Edna dealt a devastating blow to the state's case when Jacobson presented an attendance sheet and report card from the school, showing all A's, with her grandson in the process of graduating. The state had no way to rebut her testimony or the tendered documents, since the material was accurate and up-to-date.

Von, though underestimated, was much smarter than he appeared. His home period teacher admired him in so many ways. She even had a personal connection with his father. Being from the same neighborhood herself and having attended school with Hound Jr., not to mention the crush she had for the man, she took it upon herself to ensure Vonnie was marked present for every class, and prevented his grades from slipping, by keeping them marked up to A levels. When she became aware of his arrest and the inevitable trial, she visited Mrs. Edna's home (knowing where Vonnie lived) to offer her assistance.

Upon hearing his grandmother's testimony, Von glanced around the courtroom in search for the delightful school teacher. She wasn't visible, being sequestered in the witness room. However, his dad pointed in the direction was she was, indicating she was there. He understood what was happening, and took it in stride. Ms. Taymar Peterson, the woman who cared for her troubled student and had an infatuation with his father, was willing to lie, cheat, perjure herself, to save his skin. Von turned his focus to his father once more, as Hound Jr. silently indicated that they would talk later. To Von, it felt as though God himself had sent an angel to help him out just in the nick of time. All praise was due, even from a supposed "demon-boy" like Von.

Jacobson further displayed his shrewdness by asking Mrs. Edna fewer than ten questions, adhering to the notion that *less is more.*

"No further questions for the witness, Your Honor," Jacobson announced.

It was now the state's turn to cross-examine the witness.

Shapiro began with the basics. He delved into Mrs. Edna's history as a grandparent to Von and her own upbringing. He also touched on Von's school behavior and whether or not he'd ever been suspended. He had not. The overall intention was to try and draw a pattern for the jury: if Von had displayed attitude and anger issues in school, then irrespective of his grades, he could potentially become violent, particularly towards someone he had argued with over damage to his new car.

Jacobson observed the jurors to gauge their reactions to Shapiro's questioning. They were not buying it.

"If you're trying to make my grand baby out to being a poorly raised criminal thug, who can't control his anger, you may as well stop right there, sir! Seriously! Trevon ain't no killer! My grandson did not shoot and kill nobody! So please stop trying to frame him. Okay?" Mrs. Edna stated emphatically.

Upon seeing the jurors' lack of response to his actions, Shapiro realized he needed to back off immediately. "I have no more questions for this witness, judge," he declared.

"Very well. Mister Jacobson, any redirect?" Lockhart asked.

"No, Your Honor." Jacobson stood and then sat back down.

"You're free to go, ma'am. Your next witness, Mister Jacobson."

The million-dollar question for Von's lawyer was, whether to call him to speak on his own behalf or not? Alternatively, should Jacobson call at least one more witness before resting his case?

Before the day began, Jacobson successfully had Von's school teacher added to the witness list. He could call Ms. Taymar Peterson to testify about Von's character in school and on his interactions with fellow students. This would reinforce the positive outlook the jury already had of him, without detracting from it. Additionally, based on the juror's body language, Jacobson would determine whether or not to put Von on the stand.

He decided to call the teacher.

"Yes, Your Honor. One last witness," he stated.

Suspense filled the courtroom. The anticipation of whether Vonnie would be called to testify mounted. However, it turned out to not be the case.

"The defense would like to call Miss Taymar Peterson, a schoolteacher of the defendant," Jacobson said.

Ms. Peterson, initially unsure of her place, was escorted to the stand. Jacobson swore her in and began his questioning. His line of inquiry mirrored his approach with Mrs. Edna, concise and focused.

His final question resonated throughout the courtroom: "Miss Peterson, under oath, do you believe my client, Trevon Aaron Dietrich Savage, could ever become so enraged . . .

So ticked off . . . To the point that he'd shoot someone as a result of that anger?

The teacher's voice rang out: "No! Absolutely not! Trevon is one of the most kindest students I've ever had the *privilege* to teach. And I thank God for that opportunity to teach him," she declared before the court.

"No further questions for the witness, Your Honor," Jacobson said.

"Very well. Mister Shapiro, your turn to examine the witness.

Shapiro rose to his feet, proceeding with caution. He understood the importance of crafting his questions to diffuse the impact of Jacobson's previous inquiry. The damage to the state's case was already apparent, evident in the body language and demeanor of all twelve jurors, including the alternates. It seemed inevitable that the state's position was spiralling down to the bottom of a rock pit.

"No more questions for the witness, Judge," Shapiro conceded.

"Very well. You may leave, Miss Peterson."

"Thank you, Your Honor."

The teacher rose to her feet and exited the courtroom gallery, heading to the hall lobby to wait for Hound Jr. to come out. She was eager to have a conversation with him.

Meanwhile, Shapiro remained standing, ready to address the court. "The state rests, Your Honor."

Jacobson followed suit. "The defense rests as well."

Judge Lockhart acknowledged them. "The time is nearing noon. We'll take a lunch break and reconvene at twelve-thirty P.M. for closing arguments. Following that, the jury will begin deliberations. Court is adjourned,"

It was clear that Von would not be called to testify.

Chapter 27

One Hour Later . . .

The lunch hour came to an end, and court resumed session with Shapiro taking the stage for his closing argument. Despite his request for three hours, Judge Lockhart limited him to two. This was a ploy, to gain any small victory he could possibly muster up.

"Three hours is not necessary for closing arguments, Mister Shapiro. Your request is denied. Two shall suffice," Judge Lockhart ruled.

Clearly disgruntled, Shapiro proceeded with his argument. He rehashed familiar themes, but surprisingly, wrapped it up within an hour and a half. The jury appeared weary of his arguments.

With Shapiro's presentation concluded, it was now Jacobson's turn to make his final plea. He skillfully engaged the jury and the court for one hour and five minutes, bringing the time to four P.M.

Following the presentations from both sides, Judge Lockhart gave legal instructions to the jury but decided to postpone sending them to the deliberation room to vote on a verdict until the next day. With that, court adjourned for the day

****

One Day Later . . .

Anticipation hung heavy as the trial entered its potentially final day. Jacobson exuded confidence, believing the jury wouldn't need long to deliver a "Not Guilty" verdict. Following that, Jacobson envisioned a swift process to establish his client's innocence, secure exoneration, and expunge all charges stemming from the arrest. He'd received positive vibes from each juror—at least from his observation. They seemed to be leaning in favor of the defense.

"How do you feel, Trevon?" Jacobson asked, visiting him in the holding cell.

"Real good, man! Real good."

They exchanged smiles and briefly revisited key aspects of the trial. It was crucial to ensure all details were meticulously reviewed and addressed, leaving no room for oversight.

****

Three Hours Later . . .

Just before Judge Lockhart adjourned the court for the lunch break, the bailiff was informed by the jury foreperson that a verdict had been reached. Lockhart was promptly notified. Von was escorted back into the courtroom, and everyone else returned from the lobby to the gallery. Judge Lockhart reappeared and summoned the jury back before the court.

Von's heart raced uncontrollably, and he felt like a nervous wreck. His family and supporters shared his anxiety. All previously sequestered witnesses were now seated in the gallery with the rest of the attendees, those who chose to remain.

Judge Lockhart called the court to order and began her formal speech.

"I understand that the jury has reached a verdict in this case?"

"Yes, Your Honor, that's correct," stated the female clerk of the court.

"Very well. Is the clerk prepared to render that verdict?"

"Yes, Your Honor, that's correct."

"Very well. Will the defendant please stand?"

Von, Jacobson, and the two assistants on the legal team rose to their feet.

Jacobson scrutinized the jurors' expressions. They appeared stoic and hard to read.

Von briefly trembled at the knees but regained composure. His mother crossed her fingers and bowed her head in prayer as the verdict was being read.

"In the case of The State of Pennsylvania Commonwealth versus Trevon Aaron Dietrich-Savage, we the jury find the defendant, charged with the offense of capital murder—NOT GUILTY!" the clerk pronounced.

"Oh yeah!" Von shouted. "Take that, Bill! You and your sidekick!"

He had the opportunity to turn his head to have a look at the two detectives' seated on the front row that separated the prosecutors table from the gallery.

Judge Lockhart called for order, but a smattering of applause, mostly from Von's family, erupted. One juror, an elderly African-American woman, dabbed her eyes—clearly moved by Von's grandmother testimony and that of the teacher.

While one charge was down, another loomed. However, bail now seemed a possibility.

The judged concluded the trial and dismissed the jury. Von hugged his lawyers and, after a phone call to his family, was escorted back to jail.

Chapter 28

One Week Later . . .

Hound Jr.'s ambition to become the owner of a mature gentlemen's club began to come into fruition. Drip informed him that the owner of a once-popular but now mediocre strip club, was looking to sell due to old age and wanted to move on to something else. The guy contacted him to make an offer, since he and Drip were familiar with each other, and he knew Drip's financial stability and rising prominence in the Philly nightlife scene. The club in question was the *Playground Lounge*, located on 33rd and Huntingdon Ave. A legendary spot for leisurely pastime.

Drip and Hound Jr. met up seemingly at the same time to meet Karl, the owner of the establishment, and to discuss the deal. They dapped and hugged.

"What's good, fam?" Hound Jr. greeted Drip.

"I'm good, fam. How you?" Drip responded.

"I'm feeling pretty good. Real good. My boy beat a murder charge. Thanks to you. And thanks to our Savage family, for making the power moves to have success, like we always do."

"No doubt about that, fam. We did that. And we 'bout to add to the family portfolio, when you buy this club."

"Absolutely. What's good, Body? How you, bro?" Hound Jr. greeted Drip's friend/bodyguard, who drove him and provided safety while in public.

"Everything love, bro. Tell Vonnie congratulations on the *not guilty* verdict. And we can't wait to see him out here with us again," Body said to Hound Jr.

"I'll be sure to do that. We appreciate the love too, bro"

The trio then walked inside to conduct their business at hand.

It was four P.M. The music was playing softly enough for them to converse. Two sexy females danced slowly, while a handful of patrons enjoyed drinks at the bar, and a few indulged in lap dances.

Karl was in the office when his visitors arrived. One of his security men escorted them towards his direction.

"Gentlemen! How y'all doing? It's a pleasure to see you here," Karl said during their entrance. He then approached to shake their hands.

"We're good, Karl. It's a pleasure to meet you again too. This is my cousin and close associate, Cornelius, also known as 'Little Hound'. And this is our homie, Bruce, aka 'Body.' Cornelius is interested in buying the club."

Karl's eyes went from Drip to Hound Jr. He looked him up and down, admiring the fine clothing that the guy had on. Karl was in his mid-fifties, and a natty dresser himself. It always made him smile to see a fellow black brother who was equally serious about business, and good clothing.

Both Hound Jr. and Drip had on slacks, wing-tip Italian shoes, silk button-down shirts, bow-ties, and designer glasses. Dressed to impress. A code of the Savage family that they kept true to.

Body had on a black Gucci sweat suit and a pair of black Timberland boots. Karl knew then and there that Body had to be the security man of one of them.

"Nice style, fellas. Good taste!" Karl complimented them.

"Thanks!" Drip responded.

"Now about the business. Let's get down to it," Karl stated, then opened up with the negotiations.

****

After nearly an hour of discussions, they'd reached an agreement for the purchase of the building, and also the land, for $700K.

Drip was the one who would transfer the funds from his account to Karl's on behalf of his cousin, Hound Jr., who would then provide the cash back to Drip for the deal. The transaction would take place within a week. Once that occurred, he would follow this up by having the necessary modifications to of the club, to coincide with the vision he'd had in mind. The new management staff would then be hired, setting the stage for a smooth transition.

With the club deal settled, their focus turned to helping Lily launch her boutique, fulfilling her long-held desire. Vonnie's impending freedom added to their optimism for the future. Things were looking up again.

****

Meanwhile . . .
Tito had dedicated himself to following Von's trial for its entire four-day duration. His reason for doing so was the belief that his two female cousins had been brainwashed into engaging in a three-way relationship with Von. Tito strongly suspected that Von was responsible for killing his cousin, Alfredo. The Dominquez family wanted Tito to thoroughly investigate the situation and seek justice for Alfredo. Everyone, except Chloe and Rosa, desired retribution. In particular, against those who were strongly suspected.

Although the investigation was still ongoing, the homicide division had made little progress in identifying a primary suspect, let alone make an arrest. Frustrated and grieving for his aunt Adeline—Alfredo and Rosa's mother— Tito decided to take action. Adeline reached out to Nora,

Tito's mother, asking them to visit so to discuss the situation. Tito felt compelled to take matters into his own hands.

The moment Tito and his mom entered the house, Adeline burst into tears of the sight of him. They hugged, and Adeline held onto them tightly, soaking their shirts with her emotions. As they were in the midst of this emotional moment, Alfredo's daughter, baby Kylie, emerged from the toy room with her arms wrapped around a large doll her father had bought her before his death. This sight further fueled Tito's anger, and he too began to cry. Tito leaned down to pick her up, wanting to hold her for as long as they were together.

"Hey, baby Kylie. How you doing? You've been a good little girl? Yeah, I know you have. You've been a good girl for cousin Tito," he spoke gibberish with the toddler.

"Tito, have you heard anything that could bring us closer to finding Alfredo's killer? We can't rely on the police. In our homeland, vigilante justice is often faster than the legal system itself. Our family looks to you to get the justice we deserve," Adeline implored.

Both Adeline and Nora looked on at Tito expectantly, awaiting his response. Though he didn't voice it, Tito harbored resentment towards Rosa and Chloe's involvement with Von. This situation presented an opportunity for him to distance himself from them and to take more drastic measures.

"I think I have an idea of who might have been involved or know something about it. I know where to look next," Tito replied.

"But if you already have an idea, why continue questioning? You and your guys should simply take action," Adeline insisted. "Look at my granddaughter. Does she deserve to grow up without a father? Does our family deserve to not seek justice for Alfredo's death? No, she doesn't, and neither do we."

Tito now fumed more intensely.

"Look, Momma. Aunt Adeline. Here is what I know. Here is the full truth of the story . . ."

Tito told them everything, leaving no stone unturned in his revelations. His mother and aunt were completely stunned at the news of Rosa and Chloe both having a baby by the same dude. Not to mention the same guy was the one Tito accused of killing Alfredo.

Adeline immediately grabbed the phone and called her daughter. She was pissed and ready to give Rosa an earful.

Once she was done with Rosa, she and Nora planned to call their sister Zelina—Chloe's mother—to pressure her to end any ties Chloe had with Von. Tito promised that he couldn't let Rosa and Chloe continue to disgrace the family, and he vowed to take action against Von for Alfredo's death. He knew exactly where to start.

Chapter 29

Two Days Later . . .

Chloe and Rosa were together at their place, both reeling from the harsh phone calls they'd received from their mothers. They needed to have a candid conversation about the pressure they were under.

"Chloe. What do you think we could possibly do to prove to them that Vonnie had nothing to do with Alfredo's death?" Rosa asked.

"To tell you the truth, Rosa, I don't know. I really don't. I do know for a fact that you and Vonnie were together in New York at the time Alfredo went missing and was killed. I found receipts and a hotel key card in his pants pocket while doing laundry around the time."

"And I don't understand where Mommy and Tito get the idea that Vonnie and Alfredo had a problem with each other. So much so, to the point that one wanted to kill the other," Rosa stated.

"Actually, there was a situation that had happened. But it does not directly involve Vonnie and Alfredo."

"And what was that?" Rosa asked.

Chloe went on to tell the story about the robbery that took place involving Von and Cold Heart. Von had let it slip one day and mentioned to her the names of the people who knew about the business deal he and Tito had, and who was there at the shop the day he bought the product.

Rosa immediately reflected back to the day Von entered her brother's room and went through his belonging. While the police had taken Alfredo's phone from the night stand that day, his clothes, and other belongings, the rest remained at their mother's house. Rosa contemplated sharing this with Chloe, but decided against it, not wanting to disrupt their peaceful household.

"Regardless of what happened then, we're beyond that now. Vonnie will be coming home to us soon, and we have a happy home together. We can't let anyone disrupt the progress we've made, not even family, Chloe. Vonnie made our business possible; he invested the money, and we both have children with him," Rosa firmly stated.

"True," Chloe agreed before getting up to finish getting dressed for her evening out with Raul, a date she hadn't told Rosa about.

Meanwhile, Rosa planned to go out with her friend and co-worker Meadow. It had been a while since she'd been out—Long before having her daughter. She was eager for a night about the town. Their mothers agreed to baby-sit for the night, but not without a serious discussion beforehand, to recap their concerns about Chloe and Rosa's relationship with Von.

Unbeknownst to them, Tito's plan was in motion. He aimed to divide, manipulate, and conquer, to sever Chloe and Rosa's affection for Von.

Tito wanted Raul to do all he could to pull Chloe away from Von, and make her his girl all over again. "Force her back into your life if you have to," Tito demanded. "And if he gets free, you, Enrique, and Pedro, are gonna rob him, then kill that pussy! He was the one who had Alfredo killed. And we're gonna hit him back. I've got somebody on the inside (Tito was referring to the Puerto Rican female homicide detective, Corletta Santos) keeping me updated on every case involving him. So, keep Chloe close to you. That way, when we get the opportunity to pop him, we take it.

We'll always know where he lives as long as y'all two continue to see one each other," Tito explained his plan to Raul. Everything was going accordingly.

****

One Day Later . . .

Tito and Corletta met up with each other out in Atlantic City on the board-walk. They had a solid business relationship. She provided him with invaluable information on many investigations and other works that the Philly Police Department had going on. The prime topic for that day was Von, and the troubling situation he had them entangled in.

"Corletta, please tell me, how the fuck did that bum ass Savage boy beat the murder charge y'all had him pinned down on? I gotta know this," Tito demanded as they strolled along the beach, enjoying the warm spring weather in April.

Corletta shrugged, her palms upturned, then proceeded to address Tito's inquiry. "Apparently, that little fucker got more pull than we thought. All three of the key witnesses who was lined up to testify wound up getting killed off before the ADA could get them on the stand. Three vicious slayings at that."

"I read about them," Tito remarked.

"And not only that. He has one of the most expensive and elite legal teams representing him. I highly doubt that the DA's office will take him to trial on the other murder charge he has pending."

"And what's the deal with his mother's involvement? I recall something about her being implicated as well," Tito inquired.

"She is. The guy killed was an ex-boyfriend. The case was originally viewed as a justifiable homicide. But when the son fled the scene, and the mother not forthcoming about who shot the victim, that made it something more than what it was. Something to open an investigation into the family of the boy's father as well. The Savages."

"Is that so?"

"Yep. But at the same time, the ADA Shapiro does have a tendency to overreact. This could be one of those scenarios," Corletta explained. "Now you help me understand something. Tito. What's the issue that you have with the Savage boy? I don't seem to get it fully."

"We had a beef. He bought from me one day and ended up getting robbed of everything he had not long after the fact. Motherfucker blamed me, and we had a war of words. He owed me money. Eventually, the debt was paid. Then, my cousin was kidnapped and murdered. Taken from his sister's house, killed elsewhere. And as you know, dumped in a landfill. Not many people knew where they lived. Not to mention the fact that Von Savage got involved with my cousin Rosa, Alfredo's sister, then later gets her and another woman pregnant. Our other cousin actually, Chloe," Tito recounted.

Corletta was taken aback by the revelations. Tito and Von had a lot going on between the two of them.

The conversation continued as they walked.

"So, my guess is that your family does not agree with the dealings the two girls have with Savage?" Corletta probed.

"Not in the least."

"And they look to you to do something about your male cousin being taken from you all?"

"Exactly."

"But there is no one to point the finger at to get the justice you seek. And the case is cold on the legal side?"

"Mmm-hmm. Leaving me and my family emotional and traumatized by Alfredo's death, and this is why I made it my business to re-establish your acquaintance, so that we could get the information necessary on Savage, to rid ourselves of the problems we face with dude."

"Point taken. And here is what I can tell you about the Savage boy, as it relates to the matching evidence found in the case of your cousin, and the cases we have Savage on."

"Okay. Continue. I really need to know," Tito urged her on.

"Indeed, there is a connection. The same type of bullets that took the life of Kavon Lassiter and Bernard Nichols, the ex-boyfriend of the mother, was the same one that took out your cousin," Corletta said.

"How do you know that specifically?"

"Because, they're one of a kind. *Cop Killers!* Mini lead missiles known as *Black Rhinos.*"

"How the fuck did he get his hands on such powerful ammunition!?"

"That's what we're trying to determine before the feds swoop in. There's been a series of murders with the same type of ammo, and Von Savage is the only one arrested and charged with a murder involving these extremely lethal bullets," Corletta revealed.

"Von Savage?"

"That's correct. Von Savage. But fortunately for him, the jury bought what he and his lawyers had to say. His so-called *alibi* worked out. He had his grandmother take the stand and lie on his behalf."

"A heartless piece of shit!" Tito remarked.

"Of the worst kind!" Corletta co-signed. "But who the hell in power is protecting this thug bastard? Who put out the hits on the witnesses? Why is this criminal shielded? That's what we need to uncover. I did a background check on the Savage family. They wield significant power.

Tito briefly considered disclosing his dealings with Monk to Corletta, but decided against it, understanding the implications of such an act of snitching. Their relationship was built on her providing him with information, not the other way round.

"Okay. Look. Here's what I need you to do for me. And hopefully, this'll work for you as well."

Their conversation continued, with both Tito and Corletta sharing insights and strategies on how to address the problems they faced with Von. Tito sought information on when Von would be released on bail and details about his family. Meanwhile, Corletta planned to visit the county jail to interview Von, hoping to extract crucial information.

****

One Week Later . . .

Detective Corletta Santos paid an unexpected visit to the county lock-up to interview Von. Without authorization from the department or informing her colleagues Bill and Valco, she proceeded with her interrogation, a move that raised eyebrows within the precinct.

Seated across from each other at the table, Von wore the standard jail attire, and was shackled at the ankles and wrists. Corletta greeted him with a forced smile as he entered the room.

"Well, well, well. If it isn't Trevon Aaron Dietrich-Savage. The son of Cornelius Savage Junior. The grandson of the legendary Hound Savage," Corletta said.

"Yo, who you? I ain't never seen you before," Von retorted.

"It's the first time for everything, Trevon. Just be thankful I'm not the federal government."

"To be honest, that's who I thought you was. A federal agent. And you still haven't told me what's this all about? Or who you are!"

"I'm Detective Corletta Santos. From Homicide."

"And I guess your boss sent you this time, instead of 'Beavis and Butthead' to try and work a deal, huh?" Von said, referring to Bill and Valco.

Corletta looked on at Von, then smirked behind his remark.

"Actually, I'm here about another homicide you're linked to."

"Ha, ha, ha, ha! Please. Don't make me laugh more than I have to. But I'm dying to hear about this one."

"Does the name Alfredo Dominquez sound familiar to you?"

"I should've made the connection sooner, you being Puerto Rican looking and all. But to answer your question, yeah. It does. That's the name of the brother of my daughter's mom. May he rest in peace. And why you wanna know?"

"Hmm. Good question. It's rather ironic that the same bullet that killed him matched the same type that killed Kavon Lassiter . . . and Bernard Nichols."

"Okay, so, more than one motherfucker got popped by the same kind of bullets. What the fuck that gotta do with me, Trevon Savage?"

"You and him had a beef. You got stuck up for a batch of product. You found out he may have had something to do with it. You used his sister as an alibi to get away with it on a weekend out in New York. And, you had your homie 'Cold Heart' waiting for him at the sister's house until he arrived. They then kidnapped and killed him on your orders," Corletta laid out a theory based on information from Tito

Von wagged his finger, dismissing her accusations at him. "Now see . . . Now that . . . That's a tall tale, no doubt. You're accusing me of a crime of murder."

"I'm not accusing you of anything. Not yet at least. I'm simply stating the obvious."

"Who sent you, Santos? And why? Because it's clear to me, you're fishing for something," Von said. "And I see you must have had overlooked the recent *'Not Guilty'* verdict the jury came back with."

"A *'Not Guilty'* verdict doesn't necessarily mean you didn't do it. And to answer your question, no one sent me. I came to speak with you on my own accord. And hopefully, we may be able to gain a level of understanding with each other. Because no matter what, I plan to take it upon myself to get to the bottom of the Alfredo Dominquez slaying," Corletta said in an emphatic tone.

"Look, lady," Von said, rising to his feet. "The only understanding I want you to have is to never come back my way ever again without my lawyer being notified of you pulling up on me. Okay? And good luck on your investigation. Hope you find the right place to start looking for whatever it is you're seeking. Because it ain't over here with me." He then banged on the door for the guard to remove him and escort back to his cell.

Corletta was satisfied about how the brief visit went. At the mention of Cold Heart's name, she observed Von's eyes widen with surprise, a subtle indication that she had stumbled upon something. The extent of its importance would need to be determined at a later time. However, in this moment, her curiosity was piqued, and her primary objective became the unravelling of the mystery behind this "Cold Heart"—the individual potentially holding the key to everything. He was known as Vonnie's right-hand, and brought to her attention by Tito. Uncovering Cold Heart's true identity promised to unveil crucial insights.

Chapter 30

Three Weeks Later . . .

Von's lawyer, Levi Jacobson, had filed a motion to have a bond granted. A scheduled hearing had taken place, and they were now awaiting the judge's ruling on the matter. For this particular charge of murder, there was a different judge to preside over the case. The now presiding judge, a James George Willis IV, was a relatively young white male, hailing from a lineage deeply entrenched in legal authority. His father, grandfather, and great grandfather, all bearing the same name, had served on the prosecution side of the law, with two preceding Willis IV's having held office as judges.

Von found himself in a favorable position with the case, with a different Assistant District Attorney (ADA) assigned to prosecute. Instead of Shapiro, it was Jarred Marconi, the son of Raphael Marconi, and grandson of Don Angelo Marconi, all of whom were friends of the Savage family, to which Von belonged.

Prior to the day of the hearing, a clandestine meeting had occurred. Raphael Marconi, his son Jarred, along with Hound Sr. and Hound Jr., convened at a country club in Upper Darby, Pennsylvania, to negotiate. A deal was struck between the two families, involving a $350K payment to Raphael and his son, with an additional $350K to be paid upon the potential agreement being met, pending approval by the head DA. Hound Sr. and Jr. had invested heavily to ensure Vonnie's legal troubles would be resolved. At all costs, Von had to be freed, on bail to begin with, then in totality later down the line.

The presiding judge called the court to order.

"I understand that the defendant in this case seeks to be granted bail, Mister Jacobson. Good day to you sir, by the way. You care to convince me why I should accept your client's pleadings on the matter?" Judge Willis asked.

"Yes, Your Honor. My pleasure . . ."

Von's lawyer proceeded to present his case, delivering a compelling argument to the court.

Notably, the prosecution, represented by ADA Jarred Marconi, offered little resistance to Jacobson's assertions. The smooth process was attributed to the longstanding relationship between the Savage and Marconi crime families, as well as a recent deal involving Hound Jr. and Jarred's brother, Carmine. Information unbeknownst to Von or his lawyer prior to the hearing.

Bail was granted at half a million dollars then and there. Accompanying Hound Sr. and Jr. was their longtime friend and business associate of theirs, a Freddie Johnson. He operated as a bondsman. With all paperwork finalized, Von's release was imminent, pending processing at the county jail, to be completed within a two-hour window. This unfolded on a Thursday.

****

Three Hours Later . . .

Von was now a free man. He was there at his grandpop's home, surrounded by family and friends. Monyetta and Kidada were by his side, along with Lily and her close friend Tommie Slaughter. Hound Jr., Monk and another cousin, Kenneth "Kap" Savage, were all there as well. Von preferred to keep his return on bail discreet, not even informing Chloe and Rosa, as he wanted to surprise them later. He especially wished to avoid any confrontation between his three

189

girlfriends, particularly in the presence of his grandfather. He planned to contact Cold Heart later that evening.

Warm embraces and kisses welcomed Vonnie home, turning the occasion into an impromptu celebration. Pizza and wings were ordered, satisfying Von's cravings on his special day.

Grandpop Hound Sr. requested a private meeting with his son, leading them to the personal library and study room he created for himself. The add-on room held over twenty-thousand books—a testament to Hound Sr.'s love for reading and learning, influenced by his time he'd spent in prison many years prior, and that with Angelo and Raphael Marconi.

Big Hound spoke first to open up the private conversation. "First and foremost, welcome home, son. We're glad you're back amongst us. Glory be to God and his power and mercy, for allowing this to happen for us," he said, then hugged Von once again, planting a kiss on his forehead in the process.

Hound Jr. and Von had never heard the old man speak in such sincere religious tones. They were taken by surprise in the moment.

"Amen to that, Pop," responded Jr.

"Yeah, Amen to that, grandpop," Vonnie chimed in

"Now . . . grandson . . . me and your dad had to pull a few strings and go through a dark tunnel, to see you through this situation. But I want to know from you. How did we get here, son? Shoot it straight with me. Ain't nobody here but us three. I need you to be as real as you've ever been to me and your father. Talk to us."

Hound Sr. and Jr looked on at Von strongly. His eyes went from the granddad to dad then back again; he knew they were serious with him and needed to know exactly who he was trying to be and all he wanted to do in the streets and life as a whole.

"You want me to give it to y'all straight, right?"

"Give it to us straight, son. We don't want it no other way," Hound Jr. further urged.

"All my life, I wanted to be like you two," Von confessed. "The hustlers, the gangsters. I crave power; the fear in the eyes of my enemies. And the rush that I get . . . it's addictive!" He slammed his fist on the table. "I'm addicted to the streets! I don't want to live any other way. I want a name, just like you (he pointed at the grandfather) with the Original Black Mafia, and like you (he pointed to his own father) with the Junior Black Mafia. And now, me, Monk, and Cold Heart . . . have all came together to form the New Black Mafia Brotherhood. That way, the tradition continues."

Big Hound sighed. "Son, all you had to do was ask. We could have guided you in the right way."

"I linked up with Drip and Monk at the right time. I find I can relate to them more, Grandpa, because we're closer in age. I don't mean to dismiss you as some out-of-touch old guy. I knew you're retired, Grandpop, and not out here in the streets anymore," Von explained.

His father furrowed his brows, concern etched in his features. "How did you happen to be so reckless though son? The body count you've racked up, the mess you're in with all those females, the spots y'all had that kept getting raided?"

Von shrugged, offering the only explanation he could muster. "Shit happens, Pop! That's all I can tell you on that. Shit happens. I'mma do all I can to clean it up though. I now know I can't be so reckless moving forward."

"I couldn't agree more," nodded Big Hound. "We've spent over a million getting you out of the mess you've gotten yourself into. I had to pull strings to get you bail, and it'll be my connections resolving that last murder charge you're facing. I'm telling you, you can do what you do, son. It really don't make me no difference. However, just cut out the killings. You don't want the cops breathing down your neck all the time. And you definitely don't want any attention from the feds! So tighten up, son. And don't ever ask me about my connections at no time. That ain't none of your business. Oh, and one last thing, I want my goddamn high school diploma you promised me! I'm serious about it too. Now go on and talk to your dad over there. I'll use the bathroom and head back to where everyone else is," Big Hound said before leaving them to their conversation.

Hound Jr. and his son delved into various topics. They discussed the spots Von was in control over. He and his crew. The new meth connection with the Italians that the father had, and their plans for the streets. The fortunate lack of witnesses who were willing to testify against him, is what saved his ass . . . and the day.

The father and son were now making the long awaited connection that they both had desired for many years. The plan was to move forward from that day in business together, and this was what Von had wanted all along.

****

After ten minutes more in private, Von and his dad returned to the gathering in the living room. Von entertained everyone for a few moments longer before he and Monyetta made their way to the bathroom together, one that was located upstairs and was rarely used. There was a lot of space inside. Von locked the door behind them. He then walked up to her and wrapped his arms around her waist. They began to tongue-kiss passionately.

"I love you and miss you, baby," she said to him.

"I love and miss you too, my lovely sweet Monyetta."

They continued to kiss and caress each other. Little did Von know, Monyetta wanted it more than he did. Throughout the whole time he was away, she'd kept it real with him and didn't give no other dude the pussy. As for another *female*, now that . . . that was another story all by itself. But no dick had been up in her, since the last time they'd had sex.

Monyetta began to undress, shedding her top and bra first, followed by her pants and thong, which dropped to the floor. Von removed his shirt and pants. His arousal evident from weeks of pent-up desire since his time in county lock-up; drops of pre-cum leaking from his manhood. Monyetta turned her back to him and faced in the opposite direction. She then bent over to touch her toes and allowed Vonnie to have his way. No time was wasted in the moment.

Once done with her duties of sexually satisfying her man, she then took seat on the toilet to relieve herself. From there, she thoroughly wiped and cleaned with a soapy washcloth. Von then relieved himself, wiped with a washcloth, and they both got dressed,

"It was fun, wasn't it?" Monyetta asked with a smile, kissing him at the same time.

"It damn sure was, baby. You stay knowing exactly how to please me, don't you. Your attentiveness is one of the qualities I love about you. Most of all, you provide me all the peace a man can ask for."

"Aww. That's so sweet of you, baby."

They kissed again after she washed her mouth out with the mouthwash situated on the sink. Her clean up job on his cannon was superb.

"Let's head on back downstairs where the family at. I'm sure they wanna know where we are," Monyetta said as they held strong eye contact and continued to smile at each other. "And I'll deal with you about all those *baby-mommas* later, okay. Not tonight."

"Let's do that, shall we?" he said. "And thanks."

They rejoined the family, reveling in the joyous occasion of Von's homecoming. The Savage family welcomed him back with open arms, and Von cherished every moment of it.

Epilogue

Two Weeks Later . . .

Spring was in full effect throughout Philadelphia, and the baseball season was in full swing. The city buzzed with sports energy, with the NBA Playoffs set to begin by the weekend.

Von helped his dad set up his lounge after making the necessary modifications. They also discussed plans to move the product: the meth supplied by Carmine. Von had a lot on his plate, balancing the heroin business, the new venture, and recruiting new distributors. His crew was continuing to move a large amount of product for Drip around Philly and in Williamsport.

When Von left the presence of his dad, he visited Ms. Judy (Cori and Shayla's mom) to see how she was doing and to get his daughter for the week, baby Trevonya. He wanted to spend his next three to four days with the three of his children all together. (Trevonya, Talandra, and Trevon II) He gave Ms. Judy a nice amount of money for her troubles and to further take care of Cori's first two kids, his daughter, and her bills. He assured her he was getting Cori a lawyer to represent her when the time arrived to go to court. Ms. Judy thanked him dearly, gave him a hug, and a delicate kiss on the forehead.

Next, he went to see Chloe and Rosa. He'd informed all three girlfriends that he wouldn't commit to anyone, not with his legal case pending and his grandmother's health declining. Despite this, his relationships with Chloe and Rosa remained strong.

Von and baby Trevonya arrived. He had a key to the place and let himself in, announcing his presence. Rosa greeted him first, taking Trevonya into her arms. Chloe joined in, hugging and kissing him. They were expecting him already. The intent was to put the kids to bed, then get freaky for the night. This was to be their second threesome throughout the many months they'd known about their secret dealings with each other.

"I'm good. You?" Von responded after Rosa asked him how he was.

"Mm-hmm. Never felt better, sweetheart," said Rosa.

"We're so glad you're here with us again. It makes us feel good whenever we are all together—me, Rosa, you, and all our babies. Trevonya included," Chloe said, kissing the little girl's arm.

"I'm happy to know that. I gotta be a really lucky dude, huh?" Von responded.

They all headed to the backroom. Von began to undress for a shower, preparing to relax. He stowed both pistols he had on him in the nightstand drawer next to the bed, then proceeded to wash up.

****

Four Hours Later . . .

Little did Von know, two stalkers were hot on his trail, aiming to rob him and finish him off with head shots. They had great intel and stayed close throughout his day. The mastermind behind this attack despised Von and craved his demise for personal reasons. Tonight was their prime opportunity.

Von, Chloe, and Rosa were cuddled up together. A knock shattered the quiet moment. It was just past midnight.

"Who the hell could that be?" Von muttered. The knocking became insistent. Chloe approached the door cautiously, peering through the peephole.

"Who is it?" she called out.

No answer, just another knock. Hesitantly, she unlocked the door, leaving the chain latched. Suddenly, the door splintered open, smacking her in the face, breaking her nose and bursting her lip in the process. She'd hit the carpet on impact, holding her face. Two masked figures stormed in, guns drawn. They grabbed Chloe, threatening her with violence.

"Bitch!" one the intruders snarled. He then smacked the side of her face with his pistol.

"Where that bitch-ass nigga Von at?" the other spat.

They had a tinge different accent to their voice. Not black. Not white. Hispanic, maybe?

"Please . . . Please don't hurt me," Chloe pleaded between pants. "We have children here."

"What! Bitch, I don't give a fuck!"

Whop!

The more aggressive one smacked her again.

Whop!

And again.

Clutching her hair, he yanked her to her feet and put her in a choke-hold with the barrel of the gun pointed to her temple. It was a .357 Magnum. Chloe was paralyzed from fear. She'd never had a gun pointed at her, let alone point blank. She wet herself due to how petrified she became.

"What the fuck! What the hell going on!" Von said as he jumped from the bed and plopped to the floor.

Rosa made a sprint from the room they were to where the kids were located. The ruckus startled them. They were now awake and crying at the top of the lungs. All three of them.

Adrenaline pumping, Von grabbed a gun. He then cocked it and rushed over to unplug the TV. The back area was now dark.

"Von, where the fuck you at, nigga! We know you here! Huh! Where you at, nigga? Come out and play. Or we gonna pop this bitch of yours!" the one who had Chloe threatened.

His partner in crime tapped him on the arm as if to say, *Be easy. We showed up to kill him. Not her or no one else.*

They both took a look at each other. Then, the one with Chloe at gunpoint began to force her forward, a half stop at a time.

"Please. Don't hurt us. We got kids in the back room," Chloe pleaded further

"Shut the fuck up! Keep moving!" he snarled at her, gritting his teeth.

The second intruder made his way towards the dining room and the kitchen to be sure no one was there.

Rosa had been spotted by the one holding Chloe at the time when she raced from one room to the other. The kids' space was two rooms from the master bedroom; this became the focus of the intruder on where to check first.

Chloe squirmed momentarily to stall him in a way. Those kids were top priority. And she had to do something to prevent him from going their way, in order to shield them from what it was the assailants were aiming to do.

Rosa now had all three kids wrapped tightly in her arms and balled up on the floor. They were still crying.

Von was now crouching on one knee with his arm extended and aiming through the open space of the door trying to lock in on a target.

The intruder now had Chloe at the door of the kids' room; his partner was steps behind.

The one with Chloe then kicked open the door. In a moment of bravery, Chloe elbowed the attacker in the gut. In that instance, Von sprang to action.

Boom-Boom-Boom-Boom!

He bolted from the backroom, blasting like a cowboy in a spaghetti western! Chloe made it possible for him to get off good shots when she hit the dude in the belly. The lead intruder was struck by a slug.

Boom! Boom!

Von hit the dude twice more while running up on him as he was now laid out on the floor. The first round was a head shot. Von blew the stuffing out that boy's meat top. Brain splatter and skull fragments had plastered the white painted walls.

While one intruder lay crumpled on the floor, the second intruder turned and ran as fast as he could back out the front door. Von spirited towards the door to close it and lock it immediately, securing the house.

Chloe and Rosa, shaken but unharmed, held the terrified children.

"We need to call the police!" Chloe pleaded, her voice trembling.

"No," Von rasped, his voice raw with emotion. "The cops aren't an option." He then took a look down at the dead guy on the floor. Von kicked his gun out the way, then reached down to remove the mask dude had on. He was now staring at the killed hitter.

"Enrique! What the fuck!"

Both Chloe and Rosa rushed over to have a look. They knew exactly who the guy was. And now they began to realize who it was who had sent them. They looked back and forth at each other.

"Who the fuck send them at me?" Von yelled, his eyes hardening. "I'mma definitely get down to the bottom of this shit! And soon."

He then went to the master bedroom to get his phone, then returned to where they were.

"Look! We don't say shit to nobody about this, okay? Nobody! I mean that shit! Y'all hear me?"

Von demanded their obedience.

"We're not gonna say nothing to nobody, Von. We promise. We don't want to get you in any more trouble.

You've been through enough already," Rosa said, also speaking on Chloe's behalf.

Von called his dad to let him know what had happened. He would also go on to call Cold Heart too. And Monk. They needed to get rid of the body and clean up the place quickly.

Von had a good idea who the second intruder probably was and also, who sent them. He'd deal with them both at a later time.

****

Four Hours Later . . .

The cops were called by someone else. The best part about it was: no one had any idea where the gunshot came from. So, the cops could not pinpoint exactly where to go in their search. They only circled the complex two to three times, then went on about their business.

At the time that Von's dad, cousin, and homie showed up, he had Chloe, Rosa, and the kids leave and go over to New Jersey to check into a hotel until he tells them what to do next. They had plenty of time now to dispose of the body.

"Look, Vonnie. The best thing for us to do now is to hurry and get this body outta here before the sun comes up and too many eyes be locked in on us," Hound Jr. said.

"We can take this nigga up to Williamsport to the farm and get rid of him like those other motherfuckas," Monk said.

"Smart thinking, fam. We definitely won't have to worry about them being found from that point," responded Hound Jr.

They already had the body rolled up in the carpet they'd cut a portion from, and had also cleansed the blood from the wall and floor.

"Let's get going," Hound Jr. directed.

They took Rosa's car to transport the body.

When they made it to the farm and inside the hog barn, Von had the same reaction that they did when they'd first visited.

"What the fuck is that smell!" he said, then gagged and threw up.

The others shook their heads at him

"Wait a minute. I got an idea in mind. I wanna leave the nigga a present. The bitch-ass nigga who sent them clowns at me!" Von spat.

He then proceeded to act with the thought he had in mind. They tossed the body into the wood chipper once Monk powered it to life. And then, he hit the power switch to release the wild hogs to come and eat. Von had been invited to a feeding frenzy.

****

Three Hours Later . . .

They were back in Philly and on their way to the apartment again. Von had them take a detour towards a different part of town; he had a stop to make. A gift to deliver, so to speak. Cold Heart was driving.

At the point of them reaching the destination, he grabbed a hold of the gift he'd put in a cardboard box lined with a trash bag.

"Y'all hold up. I'll be right back," he said to them, getting out the car with the item.

They had no idea who lived at the nice home they were in the driveway of.

Von put the box down on the steps directly against the door, then banged on it hard, and rang the doorbell before running off to get back into the car.

"Go, go, go!" he yelled out to Cold Heart.

They then sped away.

The owner of the home—Tito Dominquez—rushed to the front door and opened. He was super pissed behind the fact that someone banged on his door in the way they had, and not there when he appeared.

"Yo, who the fuck knocked on my door like some savage animal trying to break in!" he shouted to no one in particular. He was home alone. His wife had not long left to take the kids to school.

Tito, furious as ever, had yanked the door open once unlocked; he noticed no one. He slightly stepped forward. The tip of his foot hit the box. He looked down.

"What the fuck!" he said, then began to open the top portion. Tito was already used to boxes from Amazon and Fed Ex being delivered at his doorstep. But something was different about this one. It felt eerie and odd.

"Oh shit!" he yelled. "What the fuck!"

The content in the box made him jump back; he now had his mouth wide and eyes bucked. The gift he'd received, was the head of Enrique's body. His manhood and balls having been cut off, was stuffed in the mouth. He knew then who was responsible, and also knew that he had to watch his back from that point going forward. The heat was on for him now. It was war time. What would he do?

"I knew I should've had that black ass nigga killed when I had the chance to! He's definitely gonna get it now! Most definitely will! Fuckin' monkey!"

It was about to go down. And in a major way. Only the strong shall survive.

To Be Continued . . .

Lock Down Publications and Ca$h Presents
Assisted Publishing Packages

BASIC PACKAGE $499 Editing Cover Design Formatting	**UPGRADED PACKAGE** $800 Typing Editing Cover Design Formatting
ADVANCE PACKAGE $1,200 Typing Editing Cover Design Formatting Copyright registration Proofreading Upload book to Amazon	**LDP SUPREME PACKAGE** $1,500 Typing Editing Cover Design Formatting Copyright registration Proofreading Set up Amazon account Upload book to Amazon Advertise on LDP, Amazon and Facebook Page

***Other services available upon request.
Additional charges may apply

Lock Down Publications
P.O. Box 944
Stockbridge, GA 30281-9998
Phone: 470 303-9761

Submission Guideline

Submit the first three chapters of your completed manuscript to ldpsubmissions@gmail.com. In the subject line add **Your Book's Title**. The manuscript must be in a Word Doc file and sent as an attachment. Document should be in Times New Roman, double spaced, and in size 12 font. Also, provide your synopsis and full contact information. If sending multiple submissions, they must each be in a separate email.

Have a story but no way to send it electronically? You can still submit to LDP/Ca$h Presents. Send in the first three chapters, written or typed, of your completed manuscript to:

LDP: Submissions Dept
P.O. Box 944
Stockbridge, GA 30281-9998

DO NOT send original manuscript. Must be a duplicate.
Provide your synopsis and a cover letter containing your full contact information.

Thanks for considering LDP and Ca$h Presents.

NEW RELEASES

BLOODLINE OF A SAVAGE 1&2
THESE VICIOUS STREETS 1&2
RELENTLESS GOON
RELENTLESS GOON 2
BY PRINCE A. TAUHID

THE BUTTERFLY MAFIA 1-3
BY FUMIYA PAYNE

A THUG'S STREET PRINCESS 1&2
BY MEESHA

CITY OF SMOKE 2
BY MOLOTTI

STEPPERS 1,2&3
THE REAL BADDIES OF CHI-RAQ
BY KING RIO

THE LANE 1&2
BY KEN-KEN SPENCE

THUG OF SPADES 1&2
LOVE IN THE TRENCHES 2
CORNER BOYS
BY COREY ROBINSON

TIL DEATH 3
BY ARYANNA

THE BIRTH OF A GANGSTER 4
BY DELMONT PLAYER

PRODUCT OF THE STREETS 1&2
BY DEMOND "MONEY" ANDERSON

NO TIME FOR ERROR
BY KEESE

MONEY HUNGRY DEMONS
BY TRANAY ADAMS

Coming Soon from Lock Down Publications/Ca$h Presents

IF YOU CROSS ME ONCE 6
ANGEL V
By Anthony Fields

IMMA DIE BOUT MINE 5
By Aryanna

A THUGS STREET PRINCESS 3
By Meesha

PRODUCT OF THE STREETS 3
By Demond Money Anderson

CORNER BOYS 2
By Corey Robinson

THE MURDER QUEENS 6&7
By Michael Gallon

CITY OF SMOKE 3
By Molotti

CONFESSIONS OF A DOPE BOY
By Nicholas Lock

THA TAKEOVER
By Keith Chandler

BETRAYAL OF A G 2
By Ray Vinci

CRIME BOSS
By Playa Ray

Available Now

RESTRAINING ORDER 1 & 2
By **CA$H & Coffee**

LOVE KNOWS NO BOUNDARIES 1-3
By **Coffee**

RAISED AS A GOON I, II, III & IV
BRED BY THE SLUMS I, II, III
BLAST FOR ME I & II
ROTTEN TO THE CORE I II III
A BRONX TALE I, II, III
DUFFLE BAG CARTEL I II III IV V VI
HEARTLESS GOON I II III IV V
A SAVAGE DOPEBOY I II
DRUG LORDS I II III
CUTTHROAT MAFIA I II
KING OF THE TRENCHES
By **Ghost**

LAY IT DOWN I & II
LAST OF A DYING BREED I II
BLOOD STAINS OF A SHOTTA I & II III
By **Jamaica**

LOYAL TO THE GAME I II III
LIFE OF SIN I, II III
By **TJ & Jelissa**

IF LOVING HIM IS WRONG…I & II
LOVE ME EVEN WHEN IT HURTS I II III
By **Jelissa**

PUSH IT TO THE LIMIT
By **Bre' Hayes**

BLOODY COMMAS I & II
SKI MASK CARTEL I, II & III
KING OF NEW YORK I II, III IV V
RISE TO POWER I II III
COKE KINGS I II III IV V
BORN HEARTLESS I II III IV
KING OF THE TRAP I II
By **T.J. Edwards**

WHEN THE STREETS CLAP BACK I & II III
THE HEART OF A SAVAGE I II III IV
MONEY MAFIA I II
LOYAL TO THE SOIL I II III
By **Jibril Williams**

A DISTINGUISHED THUG STOLE MY HEART I II & III
LOVE SHOULDN'T HURT I II III IV
RENEGADE BOYS 1-4
PAID IN KARMA 1-3
SAVAGE STORMS 1-3
AN UNFORESEEN LOVE 1-3
BABY, I'M WINTERTIME COLD 1-3
A THUG'S STREET PRINCESS 1&2
By **Meesha**

A GANGSTER'S CODE 1-3
A GANGSTER'S SYN 1-3
THE SAVAGE LIFE 1-3
CHAINED TO THE STREETS 1-3
BLOOD ON THE MONEY 1-3
A GANGSTA'S PAIN 1-3
BEAUTIFUL LIES AND UGLY TRUTHS
CHURCH IN THESE STREETS
By **J-Blunt**

CUM FOR ME 1-8
An LDP Erotica Collaboration

BLOOD OF A BOSS 1-5
SHADOWS OF THE GAME
TRAP BASTARD
By **Askari**

THE STREETS BLEED MURDER 1-3
THE HEART OF A GANGSTA 1-3
By **Jerry Jackson**

WHEN A GOOD GIRL GOES BAD
By **Adrienne**

THE COST OF LOYALTY 1-3
By **Kweli**

BRIDE OF A HUSTLA 1-3
THE FETTI GIRLS 1-3
CORRUPTED BY A GANGSTA 1-4
BLINDED BY HIS LOVE
THE PRICE YOU PAY FOR LOVE 1-3
DOPE GIRL MAGIC 1-3
By **Destiny Skai**

A KINGPIN'S AMBITION
A KINGPIN'S AMBITION II
I MURDER FOR THE DOUGH
By **Ambitious**

TRUE SAVAGE 1-7
DOPE BOY MAGIC 1-3
MIDNIGHT CARTEL 1-3
CITY OF KINGZ 1&2
NIGHTMARE ON SILENT AVE
THE PLUG OF LIL MEXICO 1&2
CLASSIC CITY
By **Chris Green**

A GANGSTER'S REVENGE 1-4
THE BOSS MAN'S DAUGHTERS 1-5
A SAVAGE LOVE 1&2
BAE BELONGS TO ME 1&2
A HUSTLER'S DECEIT 1-3
WHAT BAD BITCHES DO 1-3
SOUL OF A MONSTER 1-3
KILL ZONE
A DOPE BOY'S QUEEN 1-3
TIL DEATH 1-3
IMMA DIE BOUT MINE 1-4
By **Aryanna**

A DOPEBOY'S PRAYER
By **Eddie "Wolf" Lee**

THE KING CARTEL 1-3
By **Frank Gresham**

THESE NIGGAS AIN'T LOYAL 1-3
By **Nikki Tee**

GANGSTA SHYT 1-3
By **CATO**

THE ULTIMATE BETRAYAL
By **Phoenix**

BOSS'N UP 1-3
By **Royal Nicole**

I LOVE YOU TO DEATH
By **Destiny J**

I RIDE FOR MY HITTA
I STILL RIDE FOR MY HITTA
By **Misty Holt**

LOVE & CHASIN' PAPER
By **Qay Crockett**

TO DIE IN VAIN
SINS OF A HUSTLA
By **ASAD**

BROOKLYN HUSTLAZ
By **Boogsy Morina**

BROOKLYN ON LOCK 1 & 2
By **Sonovia**

GANGSTA CITY
By **Teddy Duke**

A DRUG KING AND HIS DIAMOND 1-3
A DOPEMAN'S RICHES
HER MAN, MINE'S TOO 1&2
CASH MONEY HO'S
THE WIFEY I USED TO BE 1&2
PRETTY GIRLS DO NASTY THINGS
By **Nicole Goosby**

LIPSTICK KILLAH 1-3
CRIME OF PASSION 1-3
FRIEND OR FOE 1-3
By **Mimi**

TRAPHOUSE KING 1-3
KINGPIN KILLAZ 1-3
STREET KINGS 1&2
PAID IN BLOOD 1&2
CARTEL KILLAZ 1-3
DOPE GODS 1&2
By **Hood Rich**

THE STREETS ARE CALLING
By **Duquie Wilson**

STEADY MOBBN' 1-3
THE STREETS STAINED MY SOUL 1-3
By **Marcellus Allen**

WHO SHOT YA 1-3
SON OF A DOPE FIEND 1-4
HEAVEN GOT A GHETTO 1&2
SKI MASK MONEY 1&2
By **Renta**

GORILLAZ IN THE BAY 1-4
TEARS OF A GANGSTA 1/&2
3X KRAZY 1&2
STRAIGHT BEAST MODE 1&2
By **DE'KARI**

TRIGGADALE 1-3
MURDA WAS THE CASE 1-3
By **Elijah R. Freeman**

SLAUGHTER GANG 1-3
RUTHLESS HEART 1-3
By **Willie Slaughter**

GOD BLESS THE TRAPPERS 1-3
THESE SCANDALOUS STREETS 1-3
FEAR MY GANGSTA 1-5
THESE STREETS DON'T LOVE NOBODY 1-2
BURY ME A G 1-5
A GANGSTA'S EMPIRE 1-4
THE DOPEMAN'S BODYGAURD 1&2
THE REALEST KILLAZ 1-3
THE LAST OF THE OGS 1-3
By **Tranay Adams**

MARRIED TO A BOSS 1-3
By **Destiny Skai & Chris Green**

KINGZ OF THE GAME 1-7
CRIME BOSS 1-3
By **Playa Ray**

FUK SHYT
By **Blakk Diamond**

DON'T F#CK WITH MY HEART 1&2
By **Linnea**

ADDICTED TO THE DRAMA 1-3
IN THE ARM OF HIS BOSS
By **Jamila**

LOYALTY AIN'T PROMISED 1&2
By **Keith Williams**

YAYO 1-4
A SHOOTER'S AMBITION 1&2
BRED IN THE GAME
By **S. Allen**

TRAP GOD 1-3
RICH $AVAGE 1-3
MONEY IN THE GRAVE 1-3
CARTEL MONEY
By **Martell Troublesome Bolden**

FOREVER GANGSTA 1&2
GLOCKS ON SATIN SHEETS 1&2
By **Adrian Dulan**

TOE TAGZ 1-4
LEVELS TO THIS SHYT 1&2
IT'S JUST ME AND YOU
By **Ah'Million**

KINGPIN DREAMS 1-3
RAN OFF ON DA PLUG
By **Paper Boi Rari**

THE STREETS MADE ME 1-3
By **Larry D. Wright**

CONFESSIONS OF A GANGSTA 1-4
CONFESSIONS OF A JACKBOY 1-3
CONFESSIONS OF A HITMAN
By **Nicholas Lock**

I'M NOTHING WITHOUT HIS LOVE
SINS OF A THUG
TO THE THUG I LOVED BEFORE
A GANGSTA SAVED XMAS
IN A HUSTLER I TRUST
By **Monet Dragun**

QUIET MONEY 1-3
THUG LIFE 1-3
EXTENDED CLIP 1&2
A GANGSTA'S PARADISE
By **Trai'Quan**

CAUGHT UP IN THE LIFE 1-3
THE STREETS NEVER LET GO 1-3
By **Robert Baptiste**

NEW TO THE GAME 1-3
MONEY, MURDER & MEMORIES 1-3
By **Malik D. Rice**

CREAM 2-3
THE STREETS WILL TALK
By **Yolanda Moore**

THE STREETS WILL NEVER CLOSE 1-3
By **K'ajji**

LIFE OF A SAVAGE 1-4
A GANGSTA'S QUR'AN 1-4
MURDA SEASON 1-3
GANGLAND CARTEL 1-3
CHI'RAQ GANGSTAS 1-4
KILLERS ON ELM STREET 1-3
JACK BOYZ N DA BRONX 1-3
A DOPEBOY'S DREAM 1-3
JACK BOYS VS DOPE BOYS 1-3
COKE GIRLZ
COKE BOYS
SOSA GANG 1&2
BRONX SAVAGES
BODYMORE KINGPINS
BLOOD OF A GOON
By **Romell Tukes**

CONCRETE KILLA 1-3
VICIOUS LOYALTY 1-3
By **Kingpen**

THE ULTIMATE SACRIFICE 1-6
KHADIFI
IF YOU CROSS ME ONCE 1-3
ANGEL 1-4
IN THE BLINK OF AN EYE
By **Anthony Fields**

THE LIFE OF A HOOD STAR
By **Ca$h & Rashia Wilson**

NIGHTMARES OF A HUSTLA 1-3
BLOOD AND GAMES 1&2
By **King Dream**

GHOST MOB
By **Stilloan Robinson**

HARD AND RUTHLESS 1&2
MOB TOWN 251
THE BILLIONAIRE BENTLEYS 1-3
REAL G'S MOVE IN SILENCE
By **Von Diesel**

MOB TIES 1-7
SOUL OF A HUSTLER, HEART OF A KILLER 1-3
GORILLAZ IN THE TRENCHES
By **SayNoMore**

BODYMORE MURDERLAND 1-3
THE BIRTH OF A GANGSTER 1-4
By **Delmont Player**

FOR THE LOVE OF A BOSS 1&2
By **C. D. Blue**

KILLA KOUNTY 1-5
By **Khufu**

MOBBED UP 1-4
THE BRICK MAN 1-5
THE COCAINE PRINCESS 1-10
STEPPERS 1-3
SUPER GREMLIN 1-4
By **King Rio**

MONEY GAME 1&2
By **Smoove Dolla**

A GANGSTA'S KARMA 1-4
By **FLAME**

KING OF THE TRENCHES 1-3
By **GHOST & TRANAY ADAMS**

QUEEN OF THE ZOO 1&2
By **Black Migo**

GRIMEY WAYS 1-3
BETRAYAL OF A G
By **Ray Vinci**

XMAS WITH AN ATL SHOOTER
By **Ca$h & Destiny Skai**

KING KILLA 1&2
By **Vincent "Vitto" Holloway**

BETRAYAL OF A THUG 1&2
By **Fre$h**

THE MURDER QUEENS 1-5
By **Michael Gallon**

FOR THE LOVE OF BLOOD 1-4
By **Jamel Mitchell**

HOOD CONSIGLIERE 1&2
NO TIME FOR ERROR
By **Keese**

PROTÉGÉ OF A LEGEND 1&2
LOVE IN THE TRENCHES 1&2
By **Corey Robinson**

THE PLUG'S RUTHLESS DAUGHTER
By **Tony Daniels**

BORN IN THE GRAVE 1-3
CRIME PAYS
By **Self Made Tay**

MOAN IN MY MOUTH
By **XTASY**

TORN BETWEEN A GANGSTER AND A GENTLEMAN
By **J-BLUNT & Miss Kim**

LOYALTY IS EVERYTHING 1-3
CITY OF SMOKE 1&2
By **Molotti**

HERE TODAY GONE TOMORROW 1&2
By **Fly Rock**

WOMEN LIE MEN LIE 1-4
FIFTY SHADES OF SNOW 1-3
STACK BEFORE YOU SPLURGE
GIRLS FALL LIKE DOMINOES
NAÏVE TO THE STREETS
By **ROY MILLIGAN**

PILLOW PRINCESS
By **S. Hawkins**

THE BUTTERFLY MAFIA 1-3
SALUTE MY SAVAGERY 1&2
By **Fumiya Payne**

THE LANE 1&2
By Ken-Ken Spence

THE PUSSY TRAP 1-5
By **Nene Capri**

DIRTY DNA
By **Blaque**

SANCTIFIED AND HORNY
by **XTASY**

BOOKS BY LDP'S CEO, CA$H

TRUST IN NO MAN
TRUST IN NO MAN 2
TRUST IN NO MAN 3
BONDED BY BLOOD
SHORTY GOT A THUG
THUGS CRY
THUGS CRY 2
THUGS CRY 3
TRUST NO BITCH
TRUST NO BITCH 2
TRUST NO BITCH 3
TIL MY CASKET DROPS
RESTRAINING ORDER
RESTRAINING ORDER 2
IN LOVE WITH A CONVICT
LIFE OF A HOOD STAR
XMAS WITH AN ATL SHOOTER